NOW FOR THE TURBULENCE

Books by Alma Stone

NOW FOR THE TURBULENCE

THE BANISHMENT

THE BIBLE SALESMAN

THE HARVARD TREE

NOW FOR THE TURBULENCE

Alma Stone

1983
DOUBLEDAY & COMPANY, INC.
GARDEN CITY, NEW YORK

The characters, events, and situations depicted in this novel are creations of the author, and any resemblance to actual persons, events, or situations is purely accidental.

Library of Congress Cataloging in Publication Data

Stone, Alma.
Now for the turbulence.

I. Title.
PS3569.T629N6 1983 813'.54
ISBN 0-385-18203-1
Library of Congress Catalog Card Number 82-45642

PRINTED IN THE UNITED STATES OF AMERICA
FIRST EDITION

For Mary

Do you suspect death? if I were to suspect death
I should die now.
Do you think I could walk pleasantly and well-suited
toward annihilation?

Pleasantly and well-suited I walk,
Whither I walk I cannot define, but I know it is good.

Walt Whitman: *To Think of Time*

NOW FOR THE TURBULENCE

1

Nel Thompson introduces Mr. Gamal, the young salesman, and he opens his sample case. A Middle Eastern student, with connections, he has filled his stock with embroidered blouses and robes imported from India. He lives in Nel Thompson's building, and it was her idea for him to use her living room as a temporary showroom. To lure customers, she has furnished tea and cookies. A widely held belief, unsubstantiated, is that she gets a rake-off on all sales.

"Who here has already bought Something Suitable? Let's see the hands."

Those of us who think it's stupid to ask old ladies to hold up their hands, or anything else, pretend not to hear their hostess. Others, out for whatever turns up, raise their hands. "How many?"

More than you'd think. Some have worn it, perhaps, but folded it back in the store box, smoothing it on top. Others have kept it clean—above the waist.

Residents of the Upper West Side of Manhattan, we have met to consider, among other things, burying clothes. Some of us, well aware that in the long haul it makes no difference what you wear, have come out of pure boredom. Others are interested in the right of free choice, one of the last inalienables. On the short end of the stick, the one we're on now, choices are scarce and getting scarcer. Choose your own burying clothes while you can. Keep in there exercising your rights before rigor mortis sets in.

"So exercise the right to go out naked, the way you came

in, instead of getting gypped by some A-rab hash slinger." Ida Adams looks into Mr. Gamal's glorious brown eyes and would like an affray, a test of strengths, or at the very least a lively discussion with pointing. A little fun somewhere along the line, for God's sake. You sure didn't get much at all those dry AA meetings.

Sensing himself no match for Ida, and only half suspecting what's in store from the others, Mr. Gamal refrains from answering. At Falafel, a lunch counter where he works part time, he is required to serve but not to answer old women. At home old women were not even allowed to eat in the presence of fine Arab males.

Disdained, Ida seems to doze, and Mr. Gamal now begins to show his wares. Prices vary. The Instant Cremation (Quickie) is cheapest. No one except the funeral parlor staff will ever see it, and for $4.99 Mr. Gamal is pushing soiled and fingered blouses he bought reduced from the outside racks of Mideast Bazaar, next door to Falafel. Chapel Service Precremation Attire (inside rack), casket slightly open, is more, but cheaper than the Open (All Out) casket models. As in portraiture, an allied art, unnecessary showing of hands is where they sting you. Cut your hands off at the wrist.

Mr. Gamal holds up a model. "Loose in the sleeves. Nice," he announces, and demonstrates, stretching the sleeves out widely. "Okay?" The colors, blue on blue, are lovely against his dark skin and he smiles, a purveyor of fabulous fabrics, an Eastern potentate.

The audience is on him at once.

"So who's playing shortstop she's got to have such a reach?" "Yeah, who's going to lay out like that? Usually you're all crumpled up. Dead, like an old woman." "They come in and find you. They can't pry your arms up."

He hastily pulls in the sleeves. "Okay?"

Reaction is instantaneous. "Air, air, I'm choking down here with all that dirt piled on me, with that dishrag around my neck. Let me out, let me out."

"Pull the sleeves out again," somebody orders.

Flustered—back home the old women never dared to order you; they never dared speak—he puts the blouse away and picks up another one, more popular. "Like a lounge robe," says somebody. "Now you're getting the idea more, son." "Yeah, you can relax in it. You're only dead forever." "Look, it's got pockets. You can carry your half-fare card. If you don't like the first place they send you, get a transfer for a dime."

"Try it on, Ruth. Get one for Sister."

I feel sorry for him and allow him to drape the robe around my shoulders. His hands are trembling, perspiring. The tension has made his beard grow. Trying for a light note, I execute a kind of disco Tai Chi with which I sometimes at home entertain the cats, who find it hilarious. I sway to the right and, off balance, fail to "grasp Bird's Tail." Laughs from the ladies. Embarrassment from the young man, whom I had only wanted to help. His hot dark eyes tell me: At home a silly old woman would not be permitted to embarrass an Arab. At home old women crouch back in the corner on a stack of dried camel chips and keep their traps shut.

Ashamed, I buy the robe—for me, for Sister, the cats, whomever—and jam it in the Channel Thirteen tote with my birdseed and peanuts.

Though it is not strictly a cremation crowd, several buy the $4.99 model, attractively priced. A few keep looking. "Haven't you got any single-breast models?" somebody asks. "Some of us have had the Grim Reaper, you know. That big knife comes slicing across you like you're a chicken, and you've lost it. You're lucky to keep *one*. Why should we pay for a double-decker?"

"Try Odd Lots, Lucy," advises a friend. "Poke around in Odd Lots, you might find one. Meet me Saturday and I'll go with you. Lunch at Altman's, Charleston Gardens." So Saturday's taken care of. But what about the rest of the week?

"I thought some old men would be here. Where are the samples for old men?"

"Old men are the samples, aren't they, Sonny?"

Shaking a little, Sonny Gamal, ex-potentate, packs up to go. We are glad when he hurries back to the haven of Falafel and we can get to the main business of the meeting —trying to live without dying first.

2

"Life is the greatest thing that ever happens to you. Right?"

"Right." Maybe.

"Then why do we get so tired just trying to live? Why does everything seem such an effort now, and hardly worth it at all? Why has everything begun to look like something else, or two other things?"

One purpose of our monthly meeting, DEATH IS IN, is to allow those present a sensible look at an eventual outcome some of us, treading water, don't admit or half believe yet. But how to deal with dying runs a poor second to our interest in how to handle living. The hustle for, and the high cost of, food, clothing, and shelter are prominent on our agenda; clinical and autobiographical day-by-day descriptions of the process of dying are not. Sex (before and after) is mostly skirted, but the liaison of fiscal convenience or "meaningful relationship" is evaluated and usually rejected: why trade independence for the company of a worn-out old man who wants to snuggle, can't deliver, and who's really after your social security? (Have it sent to the bank where it's safe.) Resented are our assigned roles as idiots, children, or cute old ladies. Though some present tend to act out these roles, we would choose rather to be considered as individuals, and regret that people fail to recognize that most of us are not nutty and some of us not even old.

Hooked as we are on living, though, we gear our programs to the fact that death is in the open now, The Thing. We don't practice hammering our own coffins or digging our own graves, but our exchanges are to the point, our approach informal, not morbid. Our aim is not to shock or frighten, or even to instruct, but only to familiarize ourselves with the inevitables. Praying for the old bowels and kidneys to keep signaling on time, hoping the old gray cells don't clog, we want to live decently and die the same way. All some of us want is to be left alone and to be able to keep our cats or our dogs. Here we have a chance to talk it out, to air our views, a chance some of us don't have from one meeting to the next. Though we would wish our outlook to be basically affirmative, we are practical; the larger portion of our responses is lively but far from sunny. We have a question hour, a flexible agenda, and face facts: it's a dangerous neighborhood (city, state, world) but it's home, kind of, it's where we live, sort of, and where else could we go? Where else would we want to go?

We discuss muggings first. Who's had them this week? (Purse snatching or a little friendly sidewalk bumping does not count.) Only one, Lisa Stevens: at knife point, loss of thirty-four bucks but no real injuries. Anyone else? *No?* Is this a good or a bad sign? What does it portend—more next week or less? Who's *due*—that is, besides everybody all the time, who, in particular, hasn't been mugged in six months? Di Di Wasserman, Kate Frazier, Rachel Rosen. They have all received the "overdue" printed notice—"It has now been over six months since your last appointment." Who sent it? "I called my dentist. He said he doesn't send notices to false teeth." "Yes, and it's not the oculist or the toe doctor either." Was it mailed? "It was stuck in my box. No stamp on it." "Did you call the police?" " 'Most likely a smart kid,' they said. 'A joke.' "

Who will soon be due?

If you have been mugged (the realistic word is *when*, not *if*) you are prone to knock off the passage of time as it relates to that event: three weeks since I was mugged, six weeks tomorrow, two months, four months, six months—*I'm due.* It has been just one week since my last mugging, and though it is never long out of my mind, I listen to the others now, feeling almost safe in some sort of macabre countdown.

Are there any present who have *never* been mugged? Only one, Mrs. Comer, who hasn't lived here long. She smiles diffidently, as though admitting to some gaucherie, and we read her the survival catechism.

What do you do when mugged if you recognize him/her/them?

Nothing, or they'll kill you.

Should you resist at all?

No, absolutely, even if it's your instinct to do so. Not many old women, or young ones, either, know judo in spite of the publicity the few who do, get. The widely prescribed kick in the groin? Not always within reach.

Whom do you call for help, if you can? Anybody, not that it'll do much good. Who wants to get killed trying to help old women who ought to be already dead and are no good to anybody but themselves anyway? But sure, blow your little whistle—if you can. A nice young man in the neighborhood gives them out free.

We repeat the basics: carry your keys and your name/address and money in different pockets, inside, if possible. Keep your mailbox key separate. Don't buy anything without a pocket—even Something Suitable. Look where you're going, where you've been, who's behind you, and who's coming toward you.

From muggings we go to the less personal. What insult, age-related, witnessed, heard of, or endured, burned you up the most this week? We reject as possible fiction the wilder stories—of markets where old people are bought and sold as pets for children, or gassed if not chosen, of old ones left to wait in front of stores and abandoned there. But we react hard to abuse of any kind and especially to grandparent abuse.

"That means when your children assault you with *their* children watching. There's good news, though—listen to this from an AP article. 'Most physical abuse involved neglect and blows resulting in *welts* and *bruises* rather than bone fracture.' "

"The *best* news is that children usually do what their parents do. They'll get theirs, too."

"My insult was that kindergarten sign on the wall at the Home. *Today Is Thursday. The Weather Is Warm. The Next Meal Is Lunch. The Month Is October, the Day Is* 15. Roses are red and up yours, too."

"It's just a reminder."

"Watch your step, they say, as if you're an idiot. Take care and have a good day, all you old clunkheads out there."

"It's just something nice they've thought of to say."

"It's something nice they've thought of to put you down. I'll take care and have a good day when I damn well please. Everyone treats you like you're a child."

"Not always. Some of us need a program, something to do when we wake up. Some of us even need something to believe in, something to hold on to, a little piece of property, or a memory, something to fall back on when we're blue."

"Yeah, something besides God and roaches. Or something to think, even. Sometimes when I wake up I lie there trying to think of something to think about. Why get up, if you can't think of anything to think about? But of course that's before I have my coffee."

"What burned me up was that nun in *Modern Matu-*

rity. 'Learn something new every day. Play golf, plant your nasturtiums, build on that new room. Choose, challenge, respond, appreciate!' Who the hell does she think she's talking to?"

"At least she doesn't think you're dead in the head, like two young women I stood next to at the Cézanne show. We were looking at one of his 'Mont Sainte-Victoires' when one woman said, 'Now honestly, if you didn't know he was good, would you *know* he was good?' 'Positively,' the other said. 'Amen,' I piped in. They looked at me, irked: what's an old lady doing liking Cézanne? Old ladies should stick to Andrew Wyeth."

"How about that TV show where a so-called comic asked, 'What kind of vegetable would you choose to be if you turned into one?'

"Then he changed his voice croaky, or high like a fool, the way they make old people talk, and answered himself: 'A turnip. An eggplant. Asparagus. A radish. A mushroom.' "

We are exact, and say, "A mushroom is a fungus, not a real vegetable." But we are fair, too. "At least he gave them freedom of choice."

"Which is more than I got when they put that asterisk after my name on the door at the Home. I don't want an asterisk after my name, I said. Over ninety you get an asterisk and like it, they said. So I got an asterisk." All who haven't forgotten what an asterisk is smile.

"I didn't get anything. A girl handing out leaflets on the street passed one to everybody but me." What kind of leaflets? They may have been for idiots only. "I don't care what kind they were. She should have passed me one. She just looked away and pulled her hand back like I wasn't important enough to get a leaflet, though she still had this whole pack she had to give away. Walking home, I cried."

"Why didn't you snatch one out of her hand and kick her teeth in?" Who does she think she is, deciding who gets the leaflets, just because she's got 'em in her hand?

After insults we take up rewards. "The most rewarding thing that happened to me this week was that I met a dog named Stanley on the corner and he looked right at me. That's all. Nothing earthshaking. Didn't take more'n a minute, but I sure keep going back to that corner. No luck yet, but I haven't given up." We smile at Mrs. Comer. "Stay off that corner, Stan. Don't forget you've got a permanent date for your first mugging."

"My reward was my daughter spoke to me nice, even when nobody else was listening."

"My son came to see me and didn't mention but once what a long trip it was in from New Jersey. I was so happy I forgot to remind him that if we lived together he wouldn't have to make it."

"I read in the paper what Nellie Brown, aged eighty-five, and a swimmer, said: 'I just love those flip turns in synchronized swimming.' Me, I can't even get in the bathtub anymore, but old Nellie's out there doing synchronized flip turns. I think it's wonderful."

"I saw the Rembrandt drawings at the Met. When I got home I tried to copy one, but it doesn't look quite like his."

"Give it time," says somebody and we laugh and go on to recommendations of what special art to see (Morgan Library, Asia House), what books to read (a new mystery, overrated, by P. D. James, somebody's memoir—another peep show at the Bloomsbury bunch), what's a good bargain in the stores (lettuce, 39 cents), what clerks in what stores have been polite, or rude, whom to boycott, whom to patronize, who's sick and what shall we do for them. We note then the absence of some we know who have died since the last meeting: the woman who in winter and summer walked the streets ceaselessly in her galoshes, until at last she had given out in front of Yum Yum's, nameless to us still and dying alone, though in the noontime crowd. Mrs. R., who, fighting for her stray cats when neighborhood hoodlums had fired her apartment, had died of a heart attack. Old Mrs. White, who went in her wheelchair, sucking a lollipop and masturbating like mad. Mr. Sanderson, who had just keeled over at the dinner table right before dessert (tapioca pudding). "He didn't even have time to say 'Oh.' "

"That's the way I want to go."

"Not me. Where do you think you're *going?* Nowhere. I don't want to just pop off—slump, and it's all over. I want to drag it out a little, not to suffer too much, but have a little fun, make something out of it, like changing the seasons. Noticed, I guess is what I mean. Let those mentioned in the will get busy being nice to me. Pass me the dessert. I want to have it, not die before it."

This leads us directly, or not, into wills, which we strongly suggest making—it's easier on everybody even if there's nobody and you've got nothing. We touch on suicide as common sense, as a choice (but read the label), and as another inalienable like euthanasia (be sure you're right). We assess memorial clubs, turn thumbs down on trendy tombstones, and collect inscriptions we think appropriate. Mainly we talk death out, or down—the Last Indignity, or a "delicious near-by freedom"? But we never badmouth it. We joke about it some—"Death is as grand as life," ha ha—knowing well that in the end it will not be all that amusing.

"Death is a part of living, like being born," says someone who has heard it.

"Death is a part of dying, like being dead," says someone

who has seen it. Most present have two great fears—that they will die, and that they will die alone.

"So I try to keep something breathing around me, and hope it's me."

It's clear what they mean, but how else do you do it, except alone? A loner at heart, I wonder. Surely they don't mean they want somebody to die with them. And if you live alone aren't you pretty apt to die alone?

"Oh, I've got a good undertaker. I've quit worrying," says someone.

"It's a bad arrangement, however you look at it. I'm against it."

"Put it on her tombstone: 'It's a bad arrangement.' "

"I just lay there and hope it won't happen. Then sometimes I hope it will. What's the difference?"

"A lot," says someone, me. "Live."

"What I wonder is which will get me first—muggers or cancer? Not a matter of choice, but kind of an interesting gamble."

"What worries me," says Helen Roth, "is how they'll get me out of the room with all that pseudo-art old Alex brought back from India that time he was spouting off as a government consultant. The doorway's narrow and we had trouble even getting in that old Siva statue with all those arms sticking out all over the place. If they move that old spread-out Sitting Buddha, though, and put one of the Standing Buddhas there instead, and turn me kind of sideways like this"—we watch her demonstrate—"they might be able to do it. Once I got out of bed and measured it, but then I thought, You dope, they take you out in a sack, anyway. Get around any corner. Drag you down the stairs, bumpety bump."

"Boy, that's a good one for the tombstone collection."

"Wrong." Ida Adams wakes up. "It's a natural for a

song, a perfect polka." Ida played bass fiddle in a girls' band in the thirties and her musical opinion is not questioned. "It's like 'Roll Out the Barrel.' Four-fourths time. A major."

"Hit it, Ida." With the palm of her hand Ida bops out the time on the arm of her chair. A few beat with her, out of time, and Ida quits. She had toured the whole U.S. and Tijuana too; whenever anybody gets out of time she quits. That is something she just cannot tolerate. She slumps back in her chair. The AA meetings were a drag all right, but there were a lot of good drummers there.

"So I got a load off my mind and am kind of enjoying it now, just waiting where I am. I'm sure not going, like some old sick people, to live near the cemetery so I'll be close to the hole and less trouble to survivors. That's their worry."

"You're lucky not to have any loving family hanging over you," says Kate Frazier. "Mine is just waiting for me to die at a time convenient for them. Once in a feeble moment I tried to make it for them while they were all up here together at the Independent Drillers Convention. It seemed a thoughtful thing to do, at least *they* thought so. Limited-time round-trip fares, and a big bowl game coming up down home. But when they kept calling me from the hotel—'How you feel, Cousin Kate?' 'Any change today, Aunt Kate?'—I got stronger and stronger. Why should I cut short my good life with my delicious lunches at the Oyster Bar and all my nice classes at the New School? Just so they can get back home in time for the big game and the big brag. 'Of course we were right there, honey, when she died. We couldn't leave her to kick that final goal by herself.' Why should I meet any deadlines for them? I've got two hundred and sixty-five more courses to take. I'm registering for calligraphy next time, not for obituaries."

We discuss obituaries, too, but most of us, like Kate

Frazier, are trying to stay off the page, not get on it. I am surprised when Nel Thompson corners me near the oatmeal cookies with a request. "Look, you don't have to drop any envelopes like you do for the Heart Fund, or ask for a cent. You don't even have to find a home for Jody, my dog. He's had a easy life. Just let him go when I do. Why should he live on, enjoying himself, when I'm out there floundering around God knows where?"

Nel Thompson has a good, sharp mind, is humorless and tactless, honest, straightforward (stinking, disagreeable), and invariably brings out the "you-and-who-else" in me, the kind of person you like if you can stand her. "Who else is coming?" she asks if invited out. "What are you having to eat?" We've known each other a long, long time, and I'm fond of her. I must be, because I keep telling myself so.

"Where are you going?"

"I mean die." My obtuseness annoys her and unhinges her spelling. "D-y-e."

"Are you s-y-c-k?"

"We're all sick, for Christ's sake. Some are smart enough to know it and some are too crazy. But thank God, I'm not. What I want you to do if you outlive me is just to go around and sign up people to come to my funeral. You can't depend on anybody," she says. "None of these creeps here will probably come." But why? Her eyes blaze into mine. Why, why?

Oh, for God's sake. I look away, reminded of Mr. Gamal: why, why are stupid old women against me, a fine Arab male, a prince honored in his own country? I think of his hurt, arrogant eyes, I think, too, of the old women shoved back on the turds, without cushions even.

"Why don't you get a good live-wire undertaker, like the lady says? You don't think those big crowds at funerals just happen, do you?" I try to treat it as a joke, though know it isn't. A large number of supposedly sane people worry about this: it's not only hard to die, it's hard to be properly buried. "There's plenty of planning and organization and arm twisting goes into those crowds."

"There's where you come in," she says. "If you'll do it."

She looks at me almost humbly and I'm touched. I like her. I really *do* (I think) but why, why?

"Anybody special you want me to ask? Blacks, whites, Hispanics, Chicanos, men, women, unisex? Do you have any preferences?"

"No, why should I? I'll be dead."

"So why do you want all those people there wasting time looking at you when they could be at home looking at the stories?"

"All what people? I haven't got anybody there yet."

"Is that all I have to do, then, pay somebody through the nose to come?"

She hesitates, as if some exquisite refinement of which I am too coarse to have knowledge is holding her back. But not for long. "It's my obituary," she says.

"Oh, I don't mind writing that for you."

She hesitates again, then I hear her say, "You're too wordy. You might get the rejection slip. I've written my own."

"They probably won't print it," I say with some heat.

"That's for you to make sure they do," she says. "Send it in as soon as you get the death certificate. Is it true you have to be a Jew or famous to get on the obit page?"

"Fine print or social news item?"

"Social news item."

"You have to be dead."

"A dead Jew?"

Oh, God. "It helps to be dead. How am I too wordy?"

"All that sophomoric garbage you drag into your stories, messing around with Walt Whitman. It's naïve for a woman your age to read Whitman so much. It's kid stuff. All that 'battles are lost in the same spirit in which they are won,' all that 'Smile, for your lover comes' crap. *What* lover? You mean that old bird you're always watching pick up sweet potatoes at the fruit stand? Or that renovated rooster that calls you drunk from Miami at 3 A.M. and talks about his cats?"

"How about my broken-winged jay in the park? And that pigeon that followed me home up in the elevator and hung around outside the apartment, moon-eyed, till people began to talk? And don't forget Rupert either, who comes out from behind the sink every night and referees the roach fights. How come you forgot Rupert?"

"You forget him," she says. "And those other old fairies, James and Whitman. Get with the grown-up stuff. Let somebody pin somebody down somewhere, for God's sake, even if they knock 'em out. Another thing, you put your crap in the wrong place. You should save your crap till nearer the end." Then she lets me have it full face. "No wonder you can't write a decent obituary."

I watch her stalk back to her other guests, none of whom will go to her funeral, only me. She's a pain in the butt: put it on her tombstone. All she has to do is die. I have to try to sell her funeral.

Nothing tires old ladies like other old ladies—this is for *old* people, not for *me,* I keep thinking—and, equipped with my tote bag and cremation dress, I make it to the exit. So does Ida Adams, who precedes me outside and crosses to Amsterdam Avenue. In front of the Cathedral Church of St. John the Divine a tourist is relieving himself behind a bus. His camera is flapping. Ida stops to watch, sort of beating out the time, polka. "Nice balls," she calls. He shrinks behind the bus. It will likely shake him all day and ruin his exposure of the famous Gothic edifice—601 feet long and at the transepts 320 wide, second only to St. Peter's.

But it has made Ida's day. They had probably done that a lot on the road. Passing through a town, the girls in the band, tired, half-drunk, homesick for something, would lean out the windows of the bus and give their call; if in the South they would add "you-alls" and the men on the sidewalk would flip. In the back, Ida would begin to slap the bass and the girls would ride on, pepped up, planning for the next town.

Still in polka time, Ida heads in the direction of the AA meeting. Instead of going directly home, a few steps away, I go to Riverside Drive to get Sister a leaf.

3

Most old ladies tolerate trees but don't give a damn about leaves, or anything else except making it through the day. But leaves have been a favorite with Sister since her Camp Fire Girl days, and on my bird- and squirrel-feeding visits to Riverside Drive I usually find a nice long-stemmed one to take her to stir her bourbon with.

Today I refresh myself with the keen October air and, escorted by pigeons of my acquaintance, take sights. Locusts and heavy-trunked elms line each side of the wide upper walk. When full green their delicate leaves meet high above the middle of the walk and make oriental designs on the benches below. Sparser, and golden now, these trees are lovely, but like those other beauties, the linden, the tulip, and a tree of my childhood, the tamarind, they do not bear a leaf to take home and say Look. It's the plane, the maple, and the oak, rooted in the park below, that spread their generous limbs over the wall and drop the leaves old ladies want. The maples and the planes, the latter's leaves so similar to those of the sweet gums and sycamores Sister and I grew up with, are eye-catchers, but I head for the oak. There is one that leans especially far over the wall and to which I am drawn not only by its present splurge of red but because it is also the hangout of my friend the crippled jaybird.

For safety reasons I no longer enter the park itself, and, walking by the wall now, hear a jay call. It is my broken-winged friend and I hurry to place a nut on the wall. Family man, father of many, fierce fighter for landing rights, he has been absent for a couple of days. Dragging his wing, he flies awkwardly to the limb nearest the wall and hops down to grab his nut, angling it expertly in his beak. I leave him another nut (Thanks for coming) and, practicing my new modified sidewinder I've learned from watching a Pittsburgh pitcher, throw seed over the wall for the pigeons. In a maple two young squirrels begin a contest: who can leap the farthest from tree to tree without touching the ground? I place my bet on the shy one and lose when he/she is startled by a late robin, and grounded. I throw him/her the rest of the nuts and proceed toward my main objective—a coveted oak leaf, red in the middle, russet-trimmed, and waiting for me. It is then I see my neighbor, Mrs. Ordway, approaching from the opposite direction, and speed up. Dodging a jogger—why do they have to look so pained? If it's so good for them why don't they ever smile?—I call out, "Lean over the wall quick and look at that young squirrel, Mrs. Ordway, staring at the robin. He acts surprised to see him still here." It sounds silly even to me, and Mrs. Ordway, not to be distracted by childish tricks or squirrel watching, grabs the best leaf again. "Not the brightest, you know," she says, as she passes.

Grinning like a sap—does she mean me or the squirrel?—I settle for something smaller, reach for the maple leaf, and under it find a little dead bird. Green, with a red spot on his head, he is no longer than my middle finger. I smooth out the feathers, folded neatly, as though he were planted here. His tiny claws are curled under. Did he fall in flight? Was he alone? Did he feel a moment of fright before he fell? Why didn't the others stop for him, just fold a wing there a moment and wait while he rested? What was the big hurry? Had he felt that old "delicious near-by freedom of death"? I certainly doubt it. Like Mr. Sanderson, he probably didn't even have time to say "Oh," or make his will. Just keeled over, and the others left him. We got a long way to go tonight. We got to win the West tonight. Again.

Why do I always have to find the dead birds, the little redpolls, the warblers who can't make it, and knock my heart out? Why can't Mrs. Ordway with her big, baggy tongue and her goddamned big leaf find them?

Promising him honorable burial, I pack him in Kleenex and put him in Channel Thirteen by the cremation robe. At home I'll transfer him to a flower pot with the others.

A dashed old woman with a lesser leaf and a dead bird, I watch the children in the playground. A large, white-haired old man comes, as he does each day, to throw the children in the air and catch them. The supervisors watch. Laughing, enjoying it more than the children, the old man throws them higher. They scream. Soon the supervisors will ask him to come no more. He will not understand. Now the children march hand in hand back to the day care center. Soon too, Mommy will rush in to take them home, and some look glad, but some, not yet recovered from the morning parting, slow their steps, putting off the meeting. One, evidently trying to forget—why is she always lagging? Why do I have to pretend she has to work late?—appears to have made up some secret compensatory joke and smiles broadly as he marches. All sing: "One, two, three, four. Let him doody on the floor." A group from the detoxification center watches them pass. On an escorted outing, forced, they sit close together on the benches under the trees and say little. Black and white, men and women, mostly middle-aged, they stare in front of them. A few bend over and look at the ground where the children have walked. When a large black man beckons, they rise to go back to the center. They do not march but walk closely together as though for protection. Then they, too, disappear.

Alone on the scrappy island of grass at the top of the stairs, I spy a pencil stub by the statue of Samuel J. Tilden and bend to pick it up. Three boys jump from behind the statue and pull at my bag. One wields a broken bottle as weapon, but, an automatic fool, I pull back hard on the bag. Without warning, as suddenly as they appeared, the three run off. Lucky to still have it, I catch my breath, then shake the birdseed out of my shoes and walk toward Broadway.

A dog does his business on the sidewalk and watches his girl owner do a messy scooping job. He looks up at me, embarrassed—for her? for himself? for me?—and, glancing away to a sign on the post, I read about Cindy, an aged beagle, lost or stolen here a few days ago, and on medication. A *Please* with phone number and promise of reward, no questions asked, is underscored. A rat scurries through the leaves, one of a large colony that thrives here. It is possible that I feed them (people have said so), but unintentionally.

At the bank there is a crowd as usual at the glassed-off portion near the door. Here it is all computers, but money has been seen coming out of those narrow slots. They say it is real. A confirmed teller woman, I would not know and leave it alone. Not so Mrs. Reeder, whom I speak to now as she comes out the door. I am Miss Reed. She is Mrs. Reeder. We have finally spoken after years of passing on the street, eyes averted, mouths uncertain, and know this about each other, but not much more. "Why, hello, Miss Reed." "Hello, Mrs. Reeder." Shall I engage her for Nel Thompson? Not yet, I decide, and we pass. She is well-to-do, at least she goes into a well-to-do-looking apartment house, wears high boots, and looks straight ahead. I watch the ground a lot, as if searching for something I haven't got, like a big leaf or a pencil stub that will write a decent obit. I have a cremation robe, though, and a little dead bird, and in the store where we both trade am a bigger buyer in the cedar-chip cat litter department. But she is well known too, large on leeks, and greeted by clerks.

In the middle of Broadway a woman on one of the benches rises and hits me hard on the arm. She is unknown to me, demented, one of the hapless, hopeless single-room occupants, and though a second ago the crossing was crowded, I am, as in the park, momentarily alone with an assailant. I give her a wide berth, get too close to the oncoming traffic, am nearly nipped by a car, and jump back. She strikes again; three of her fingers are missing and this time it ruins her aim. Trying to feel sorry for her, I risk the traffic and cross. She waits for the next victim. No policemen are around.

At the fruit stand I pick out some small okra and a perfect persimmon, the latter large, on sale, and no relation to the wild country type I grew up on. It is overripe, in the opinion of the too smart Greek owner, who thinks he knows persimmons better than I. I smile brightly, paying him; he shrugs. He does not speak to old ladies, even those who smile brightly; he speaks only to young ladies. Old ladies get shrugs. I shrug back and, casing the street for newsy items to stash away for Sister, head for the bookstalls.

This is Columbia University turf and there are three stalls within that many blocks. More rewarding than church or Off Broadway, bookstalling is cheap pastime for me, a pushover for the street fair, the block party, the sidewalk market. A girl has recently been killed by a falling stone from one of the old buildings, her parents are suing for millions, and the sidewalk in front of the stores is now covered with precautionary protective roofing. The side street on which we first lived when we came to New York is corseted in steel. Held up by jointed rods, the board and tin covering makes a gloomy underpass, a depressing walk even in daytime, somewhat like wartime blackout, or the river Styx, and to me it is as dangerous as the falling stones. Homemade signs of the store owners caught in the squeeze are the only comforting touch.

To get as far as possible from the steel supporting rods, I walk close to the curb and, turning at the stall, am almost knocked down by three running boys. Are they the same ones who assailed me? I cannot tell. They have pushed over the outside stalls and the books, mostly for children, lie on the sidewalk. A girl clerk is picking them up when a young man stops. He cannot believe what he sees.

"You mean them boys turned this over deliberately?"

The girl nods.

"I think that's terrible. I'll help you," he says. "Just deliberately did it. Wait till old Pard props up his bottle." He steadies his bottle carefully against the fireplug and picks up a pile of books. "Load me up," he says and the girl stacks the pile higher. Now and then he stops to look at a picture on the back, or read a title. He has on a clean white T-shirt that says *Save Our Libraries,* and blue and white canvas shoes. A navy-blue tote bag is slung over one shoulder. *Books Are the Enrichers of Life,* it declares. Sometimes the man smiles a little, reading, then goes back to stacking the books on the stalls. Feeling good, he takes his time, comparing pages.

"Come on, for Christ's sake," says a woman, passing. "You're blocking the sidewalk."

"Just a minute, lady."

"Goddamn children's books." The woman grows more impatient. "Who needs 'em?"

"Little children need 'em, ma'am," says the man. "Just wait till we get all the little books put up."

"Be sure and get 'em in alphabetical order," says the woman, seething.

"No, I'm doing 'em by title, ma'am. These is little children's books."

Now I get in the act. "You should do them by author, whatever they are," I say, handing him a book.

He looks at me a moment intently before we both smile. "Thank you, Mama. I'll remember that. This looks like a little book I'm gonna buy." Picking up his bottle, he goes into the store. In a few moments he returns with his purchase, drops it in his tote bag, and goes on down the street. In the middle of the block, he turns back and waves. I watch him go down the street. Does he have a slight limp, or has he drunk too much from the bottle?

In the other stall I find an *Animal Farm* for me and, for old times' sake, a worn, pencil-annotated paperback of *Leaves of Grass* for Sister. On the way home I stop at the discount drugstore for transistor batteries and, crossing Broadway, at Mama Joy's for cheese, black bread, and a carton of Kool Super Lites. Now there's only one more stop, the Registrar.

Here is our succor and our lifeline, the courthouse square of our street. More specifically, it is the source of our cash and our booze. Narrow in physical concept, it is wide in heart and in good deeds. Julio rushes to the front, smiling, willing, Chris waves from the wine racks, and in the back Kirby, the gracious owner, loud and friendly, sends cheery greetings to Kate, my sister. Her name is Keith, but he will not believe it, even written on weekly checks, and alternates between Kit and Kate. But when Sister had her first stroke and I could not lift her, it was Kirby who sent help.

"Tell Kitty to come see us," he calls now, and, making out the check simply to "The Registrar," implying a transaction with academic overtones, I wrap the bourbon in the cremation robe, and loaded like most old ladies, walk down the side street toward home.

Many live on superior avenues with better pavement and costlier façades but few if any can boast, or perhaps would even care to, of a statue of an almost-President at one end of the street and a monument to a saint at the other end. Tilden (I trust the people) is seldom noticed except by dog walkers, bird feeders, waiting thugs, and winos who lounge at his base. But call it what some have—the world's largest unfinished Gothic cathedral, architectural achievement, monumental mistake, slum landlord, spiritual haven, community center, where they had the funerals for Duke Ellington and Fiorello La Guardia (at different times)—St. John the Divine occupies a tree-clustered block fronting Amsterdam Avenue and is an impressive asset to our humble street. Strong on Jesus, Solar Energy, Earth and Ecology, Performing Arts, Craft Fairs, Tai Chi, and AA, it is definitely part of our lives.

Outshone, but sturdily constructed in the twenties, the buildings on our street have so far escaped the iron-rod treatment. Except for the nursing home and a vandalized and abandoned squatters' quarters, most are now owned by Columbia, though Sister and I remember when they weren't and when there were awnings and elevator men. But we also remember when there were no trees in front of the houses. Ours are ginkgos, lovely little clowns with leaves like tiny fans that are as yellow and autumnly handsome now as any rural maple's and making a statement (Good-bye) just as profound. But I would never dare try to pass one off on Sister.

Large Louie, sitting on the stoop of one of the several houses he supers, watches me approach. He dangles a plump North Carolina leg.

"Got a leaf, huh?" Stolid, friendly, he smiles. His face is tight and fat and his hair is beginning to gray. "Yeah, I got a leaf." "Mrs. Ordway's got a bigger." I stop to explain it to him again. "It's not the size, it's the quality that counts." I find myself saying this an awful lot lately, almost defensively. Why? I have a perfectly good leaf here, and a lovely little dead bird, why do I apologize?

I look at Louie's big arms. "Quantity is not everything, you know. In fact, it's just a darn nuisance." Whatever it is I mean by this, Louie does not believe a word of it—super of five houses, why should he? Temporarily bested, but not permanently beaten, I go on and, a few steps from our apartment house, get my key in hand. If you have to look for your key before you get the door open, you could be stabbed, boxed, have your serial number erased, your engine removed, your small parts sold for junk, and the remains, if any, shipped to South America. In front of the house, no name here, just a number that in bolita often comes out lucky for one of Sister's intermittent numbers-addicted nurses, I look around, making sure no muggers are near enough to reach, rob, and kick me in the stomach as the undistinguishable young man was a week ago before, off guard, I could apply my key to the outside lock. No need for the key today, though; the lock is broken again and Mr. Loewenstein, our patriarchal Russian friend who has lived on the same floor with us since 1940, is sitting on the steps with his nurse, taking the sun. He kisses my hand and goes back to his newspaper, *HOBOE*. In the lobby, not always clean, I push the elevator button and, while waiting for its slow descent, collect the usual pile of mail, make a hasty run through the first classers, and, alone on the hall bench, read the news on the Bulletin Board.

The house is old, fireproof, full of memories, and though not the only building of which we have memories in this city, has been our home for forty years. The failing parts that plague old houses—the elevator, the front door, the plumbing, the boiler—are reflected in the messages on the board.

Please fix our toilet. It flushes continuously. The Huangs. Apt. 6B. Chinese, scholars, they have spelled it right, too, or at least I assume that it never stops. *Clean the filthy floors. Fix the lock. Wash the halls.* Someone begins to hurry down the stairs, almost running. Alert, I wait to see who it is. A new mugger? No, one of the many students this time, young and late, who cannot wait for the elevator.

A door opens and Mrs. Harkness comes out of her small first-floor apartment. Ronny, her dog, tries to follow. She closes the door on him and walks slowly to the mailboxes. The blue eyes are smiling, faded, and she bids me a pleasant afternoon. Her hair, wispy, is pulled back of her ears. She has trouble with her mailbox key. Ronny keeps barking. There is no mail, except Con Edison's bill, and she goes home to Ronny. In the doorway he jumps, she puts her arms around his neck and hugs him. He quits barking and she closes the door. I go back to the Bulletin Board. *Get rid of that smell in the lobby,* someone has written.

The elevator arrives and I check the light to see if it's going to the basement (never go to the basement on somebody else's light, especially if the front door is unlocked) and the mirror to be sure no one is hiding in the corners. The memory of my recent attack fresh in my mind, I do not relax. Who *will* "the perpetrator" be this time? One of the delivery boys who speaks so pleasantly of the tip and the cats, but who looks around as though getting the lay of the butcher knives and the ice pick? Will it be one of the mental patients housed in the neighborhood, one of the single-room occupants who crowd the Broadway benches? Or one of the Con Ed meter readers, the 8 A.M. young men who shout so loudly in the hall, bang so furiously on the door, stride so arrogantly through the room, and cannot read kilowatts straight? Why do I feel that I will know him?

I take a chance and start my ascent slowly and alone to the seventh floor. The trip is a real gamble for which you should take out insurance. The elevator has a varied and temperamental performance record. It stops between floors, will not move at all, will not stop on certain floors, or stays stuck in the basement. Today I am lucky. It gags once between the third and fourth floors—danger floors for stickups—but when I push the button urgently it pokes on. No one stops me en route, sticks a foot in the door, and robs me as someone once did. Kicked in the foyer, robbed in the lift, stuck between floors, and punched in the park is the way Sister and I, trying to laugh it through, sometimes describe my encounters (to visitors' shocked murmurs of dismay).

I open the door (three locks) and enter the small alcove. The rent-controlled sun is still streaming through the south windows—another reason we stay here. Sister is on the sofa busy talking back to a TV ad and does not hear me. But the cats, listening for the elevator, meet me, too excited even to investigate my tote bag. A notice has been shoved under the door, like the rent bill or a cable TV offer. But it is neither. I conceal it with the rest of the mail and follow the cats down the hall. Something more pressing than mugging is up.

4

And I think I know what it is—a little black mouse is in the toilet bowl. He is an expert swimmer, splashy, with a good breaststroke and fine coordination. The cats, dedicated water watchers, are unwilling to pursue him in his present habitat but plainly expect me to do so. Standing in the doorway, they block my passage from the bathroom. The mouse looks up at me, wet but confident. We are not unacquainted, and have an understanding concerning cats.

Martha gives me an impatient tap on the leg; her claws need cutting. "So if you're so sure that's a mouse in there, where did he come from?" The cats look at me the way Mr. Gamal had when I fell off my Tai Chi; the question is too dumb to fool with: he rattled too loudly in the sack under the kitchen table (I heard him earlier in the birdseed) and they ran him out. He took the first turn he could find, a sharp right, and jumped in the can.

Or did he come through the drains? Martha, big, beautiful, slower than Evelyn, stands on her hind feet and looks again, her stomach white as the marble, which is getting kind of yellow and cracked. I pull down the lid of the toilet and search for a container. In the kitchen I find a convenient syrup bucket, shake out the roaches, and punch holes in the lid with the ice pick kept hidden in the back of the kitchen table drawer with the butcher knives.

Locking the cats out of the bathroom, I lift the toilet lid; my little friend welcomes me with a burst of aquatics. Nellie Brown, aged eighty-five, has nothing on this mouse; he just loves that synchronized swimming. Round and round the pool he goes, flipping and turning. An admiring roach pulls up in the slow lane and we watch him together. His timing is perfect, his inhale and exhale effortless, his execution full of grace. We cheer him on, and, over-reaching, he tries for a double flip, loses the rhythm, and flounders. Begging his pardon, I scoop him into the container, clamp down the lid, and push it behind the Clorox; no need to excite Sister with news of our visitor.

Opening the door, I pick up the leaf and skid up the hall on the persimmon. Banned from the bathroom, the cats have done a thorough scatter job on the tote bag, and at a discreet distance follow me to the living room, not sure they haven't gone too far this time. But dodging muggers and joggers, picking up leaves and pencil stubs, entertaining bored cats have kept me supple if not svelte and, rescuing the bag's contents, I display the modest maple. "Look at this pretty leaf."

Sister is busy rebutting a do-good TV ad: "The next time your wife reaches for a cigarette, give her a kiss instead." "And give him a sock in the jaw," she says, lighting up her favorite brand. "So who did you old ghouls kill off today?" Sister treats our meetings lightly. She has been mugged only once and that on the very same day Edmund Wilson was impolite to her at the Princeton Club Library and she let him have it: she plunked that book down so hard in front of him he almost spoke to her, an incident that in her opinion takes precedence over the mugging.

"And what are you going to do about that big black rat back there when it jumps up and bites you on the behind?" She picks up the leaf and smiles. "It's beautiful. Little, though. Who beat you to our mighty oak again?"

The cats come in a body to petition me: it's time for their run down the outside hall. Some count this a danger, leaving us sitting ducks for prowlers: Don't you know somebody's going to grab those cats, push their way into your apartment, shoot you, steal your "All the Way with Adlai" ashtray, and smash all that fake piny-woods cut glass? But to Martha and Evelyn, limited ladies from Bide-a-Wee and named for the young women who chose them for us, it's part of the afternoon program, essential to the Happy Hour. No kin, diverse in skills and temperaments—Evelyn can rip up a sofa quicker, but Martha can demolish a plant faster—they now run like ponies down the hall, Evelyn, slim and shy, for the fun of racing, and Martha, who loves meeting people, hoping to slip in somewhere and have a surprise visit with a person. (Squushed in the cages at the shelter, it had all been cat, cat, cat, spay, spay, spay.)

I prop the door open with the big emergency flashlight and take the packages from the desk to deliver them. In addition to keeping duplicate keys for our neighbors, we're a halfway house here in that we keep packages the postmen and UPS leave with us for tenants not home at time of delivery. It entertains the cats and presumably helps the deliverymen who, though double-parked and in a hurry, are supposed to leave the tenants notes. This does not always happen and we are left holding the packages. In one for the Huangs Martha has chewed an exploratory hole, which I now attempt to paste over and if contested will blame on the deliveryman.

Sister calls the cats "those stuck-up priss-ikes you brought in here to ruin our last few days together," but she's nice to them and, if she remembers, always goes "Ssz ssz" in a civil manner. Today she waits for us on her walker while Martha and I make a few nearby deliveries. No visitor, Evelyn waits with Sister. Most recipients are grateful. Jenny, the architect, thanks us for the book on interiors, though if we had brought it sooner she could have sent it back. Emily Huang is glad to get the bean sprouts and, though she does say "finally" (sprouts are breaking through the hole Martha chewed in the box), is too polite to mention the paste job but not too polite to block the doorway against Martha's intended entry into her apartment where, unbidden, Martha had once devoured the best prongs of her fern. Whereas ours is Old-Lady Shredded with Peeling Paint, the Huangs' decor is Hanging Fern in Oriental Setting. The Flushing Waterfall in the background has somewhat broken the timeless quiet of the peaceful scene (we can hear it from the door), but Martha tries again to dodge past Emily and, unsuccessful, follows me upstairs to Eddie Fuller's.

Eddie welcomes us and the package from North Carolina, which I suspect from the grease spots seeping through the wrapping is country bacon. When Eddie is on vacation I take care of the plants and his tropical fish, who have a fickle filter but a wafer food Martha enjoys; and now, on the excuse of saying hello to our friends, Martha and I hang around the tank a minute or two listening to the gurgle, gurgle. Eddie "takes care" of his hair, drinks only beer, and on weekdays drives for a furrier. On weekends he is reed man with a combo specializing in club dances, weddings, and anniversaries. He is too sharp to open the package in my presence and begins practicing on his saxophone as soon as we give up and leave.

Waiting for us in the hall, Sister thrusts her head forward and goes "Ssz ssz." But there is no pep in it. On one of her TV programs today she has heard a woman panelist say "quantify" and it has drained her energy. Confused and unsteady, she pushes the walker in our way. We shift gears a few times till I say, "Sister, why don't you go look at your leaf?" She accepts the suggestion without balking (she *is* tired) and heads back to the apartment, closing the door when she meant to open it wider, locking us all out when she meant to go in, a mistake Evelyn would never have made.

Monica, our friend in 7B who keeps a set of our keys and is nice to the cats, is downtown looking at styles. Eddie Fuller, who has another set, cannot hear my urgent knocking over the sound of bacon frying and saxophone tooting. Large Louie has to come with his big duplicate key and let our little entourage in. Used to intricate maneuvering on the busy street, he steers us in as though we were small, inferior cars.

"Got a big cat, huh? Mrs. Ordway's got a bigger." I bring out the tip; Mrs. Ordway's is bigger, I see from the look in his eyes, and close the door from the inside.

Now we are ready for our quit-thinking-and-start-drinking hour.

5

Can two cynical old optimists sustain the intellect on sympathetic vibes from the Metropolitan Museum, the New York Philharmonic, the New York *Times*, Channel Thirteen, a house full of books, and two cats so cultured they cringe when you scrape the toast?

Can a lively interest in politics, sports, and the manufacture of Worcestershire sauce suffice as seasoning for the human spirit?

Can an active sense of humor and a few privately held beliefs supplant the claptrap simperings of the healing ministry and the religious gibberish of Original Sin and the Holy Ghost? (Everybody believes in something—a hot bath, a splint for a bird's wing, the right not to believe in *any*thing.) Can the glorious church music justify the meaningless meanderings from the pulpit? Can the mighty organ drown out the off-key croak of underpaid altos? Are only cowards religious and only fools non? Where do the "good" people come in? Can a stroll of communion among the birds and the trees temper sorrow and assuage affliction? With no belief in religion, when tragedy strikes, when sadness overwhelms, when "tried" beyond endurance, do we pray? If so, to whom, or to what? When you lose your salt and your firewater, where do you turn—within, without, up, down?

Can questioning everything resolve anything?

Nobody ever asks Sister and me these trumped-up questions, the answers being no one's business but ours and of interest to no one but us, and we ask them of ourselves only when bored or when buoyed by the libations of our Happy Hour. We make no large matter of it then: a simple "yes" when a "no" doesn't fit, a "maybe" or "why not?" if there's a reasonable possibility, a "don't know" for the imponderables. We say "Thank God" when a sick cat is made well, when a replaced fuse turns darkness into light, but we pay the vet and we tip the super. Concessions we have had to make, surely. Sister doesn't go out anymore, I seldom at night, and to the parting promise "I'll be back" now add "as soon as I can." I talk to myself more on the street instead of in empty elevators where I formerly held forth, and we neither of us remember the way we used to. We both say "probably" a lot and have never quit asking "Why?"

We've cut down on the salt since Sister's stroke, and on doctor's orders her drinks are getting weaker and weaker. But we have not yet fallen for the white wine cop-out, nor would we ever consider that other great surrender—the move to California. Our defections are minor and, except for blank-outs on dates and names, are mostly physical, not of the head and the heart, where it counts.

Disasters narrowly averted, deaths deferred, muggings avoided we take as they come. For the reverse we do the same. If we pray, it is an automatic reflex from a Methodist childhood, "Thank God" an expression like "Gesundheit." Just because we're old, we don't have to be religious. Stumbling, but stumbling on our own, we don't give up and we don't give in—yet.

To be even part of a whole person (or so some smarts has posited) each of us must have either sex, books, booze, or religion, and ideally all four, with a side order of bread. Though some say they have the first every morning with the *Times* and the last, like the Huangs' flushing toilet, continuously, Sister and I, far past any longing for either of these two, have settled on the *b*'s. A retired librarian and a failed writer, we are not old crocks, we are just people who like to drink and to read, and who've gotten older doing so. We didn't plan it that way, as we didn't plan spinsterhood, cataracts, hardening of the arteries, and that ubiquitous kiss some misguided dimwit teaches otherwise nice kids to plant on old ladies.

Small awards in our chosen fields have been ours, as have romances ranging from the tepid to the absurd and not worth recording here. Sought out somewhat at home but not much abroad, we have not purposely aimed our lives toward the single state but, rather, thought of marriage as always in the "tomorrow" stage when something better was bound to show up. Though we loudly proclaim the joy of coming home to cats instead of to old men, our not marrying, or, as Nel Thompson downgrades it, our *failure* to marry, was as surprising to us as to our multitudinous family of begetters.

The sneaking years have brought us a clear message: no matter how artful we have become in dodging the old-lady kiss (Sister more so than I, feigning a monstrous fatigue at moment of contact and letting her head droop, out of reach), we could not dodge old age. Booze we embrace as a defense against the above and all other insults, intentional or not, that come our way as septuagenarians' due. (Why do they always plop a baby down in your lap?) As we haven't lost our taste for baseball, spoon bread, Henry James, or Whitman, why should we not stand fast for bourbon?

From the kitchen I roll in the rickety ersatz bar that Margarita, our cleaning Peruvian friend, found in the basement, discarded, we imagine, by a vacating Columbia student who had found it in the basement. Evelyn hops on for the ride up the hall, draping herself gracefully around the glasses, one Polaner blackberry jelly and one good crystal, last of an old chipped line. Martha, crouching behind the door, waits to knock Evelyn off. I venture a song: "Here She Come—s, Miss A-mer-i-ca." Martha strikes and misses. Evelyn clips her one. "Scat, cat," says Sister, "get your tail out of my drink." She tries to reach for the jelly glass, of a darker hue than now allowed her, but, outmaneuvering, I hand her the other and pass the cheese, hot marrow, black bread, and crackers. Evelyn and Martha each get a thrown shrimp. Leaping, they catch them like professional outfielders.

I ease back on the sofa and render the first of my news items. "There's one old robin that hasn't gone South yet." No need to tell her of the dead bird who'd started and, awaiting burial, is now in my tote bag with the cigarettes I won't produce unless asked.

"Again? Quo animo?" Sister, who has been a reference librarian, must always be in the forefront with the news and when told something usually exclaims "Again?" as if she had heard it long ago, or certainly long before you had, and in another, much larger country. (If you had heard it first, it probably wasn't true.) The Latin throw-in is to remind you to whom you're talking—Miss With-What-Intention, the classics scholar. It is also a delaying device to cover the fact that she has momentarily lost track of the subject under discussion. She sips her drink now, mostly water and ice, scarcely colored. Something about it, the taste, peeves the hell out of her and tunes her back in on the robin. "Probably going to hide out so he can pop up and call himself the First Robin of spring. Well, I've got news for him. There's not just one of anything. Another will show up, sometimes two or three. It'll show up in some damn book somewhere."

Reference work has taught Sister to question most answers, distrust most claims, certainly the First and the Last of anything, and, along with monumental self-assurance and a rather positive way of speaking, has left her with a poor opinion of the verities and most everything else with a capital letter. Illness and frustration have not sweetened the salt. She gives her walker a swift kick now and winces; she has hurt her Tamarind, a big toe wounded in childhood.

I try again. "The shopping bag lady in front of the bank's got a new travel sticker on her bag."

"Loonyville?"

"Aix-en-Provence."

"I've been there." A drop of bourbon clings to her leaf. Sister licks it off. "This leaf is spitting on me," she says, ready to fight.

"Spit back. You've been to Aix-la-Chapelle." This is pretty daring. Sister does not like to be corrected.

"So what's the difference?" This is something she'd have never said at the reference desk or before her arteries got hard. "Anyhow, you don't know everywhere I've been or everything I've done. For all you know, I may have been married six times and run a profitable little illegal business on the side. I may have once had thirty-five girls working on call."

"True." I look at her and hope she has but can't figure out when or who it could have been, unless the latter were those unfortunate young women in cataloging she'd kept on the run. She puffs on her cigarette—cautioned, she still smokes a pack a day—and a little needed silence passes between us. Always the mighty mite, salty and sharp, Sister still has the look of a girl about her—if you don't see the wrinkles and the sick eyes. Her front teeth formerly sported a protrusion, making it difficult for her to close her mouth, but somehow, instead of giving her a look of adenoidal idiocy, it gave her one of childish expectancy or complicity. Her dentist has faithfully recaptured this look in the laboratory.

"What the hell does Aix mean anyway?" She rattles the ice in her glass; her hands shake. "I've forgot."

"Eggs?" I say, unwilling and too smart to give the right answer (and not really knowing it) when she, the philologist, could not. Encouraged by her response, more of a giggle than a laugh, I push my luck. "Bart Raither stood right there in the store and picked up exactly two pounds of sweet potatoes without weighing them."

"Again?"

"Yes, and that shitty clerk just shrugged. Didn't even congratulate him."

"He probably does it with a computer." In her prime Sister could pick up a pack of catalog cards and give within three the correct number in it. Now look what she's stuck with: an empty glass. She rattles the ice again: Get busy. I work on our drinks and declare: "The secret of success is constancy to purpose." Short on theory, long on opinion, we now engage in what passes between us as intellectual interplay. "The secret of success," says Sister, "is mowing down everybody else who gets in your way."

"But who said it?" I knew who said it. I'd been to our savings bank and read it off the wall.

"Elbert Hubbard."

"Disraeli."

"Well, they're both saps," she says and adds, as she sometimes but not often remembers to do, an incredibly immodest "In my opinion." Then: "I never guess saps." Nor does she like to miss. "Give me another one."

It's a game we play when low in adult entertainment. I choose another quote from the wall, too high for me to have got the author's name. "Provision for others is a fundamental responsibility of human life."

"My hind foot. I'm spending my wad while I'm here." Sister and I live on our social security and Teachers Insurance and Annuity Association checks, with padding from Texas Instruments dividends, and while not entirely threadbare, have to be careful spenders. "I'm not leaving my savings to cats, no matter if Woodrow Wilson did say it."

My attention wanders. Had the cats really chased him out of the birdseed or had he come down the drain? I keep hearing the roaring water in the Huangs' apartment, with the toilet flushing, flushing, and the little mouse tumbled and buffeted in the waves, ruining his coordination. And could we expect more than one mouse? Were there many more, tossing, tossing in the toilet? Were they doing it all over town? Or only on the Upper West Side? Or had he come through the unlocked lobby door? Why had he not rung? Because the intercom is broken.

"Again," says Sister, out of the blue. The Happy Hour is waning. I bring out the new paperback and put it in her hands. "Who wrote it?" she asks.

"Whitman."

"It says here Cookie Rothberg."

"She used to own it. Whitman, your old friend, wrote it."

"*Your* old friend, you mean." She hands me back the *Leaves* and looks around for livelier diversion. "Any mail besides begs, bills, and rejection slips?"

I produce the mail and we divide the begs into Yes, Maybe, This Is Ridiculous, Again?, and NO; our modest little charities (children, the disabled, the endangered) YES. Under bills we discuss Con Edison, outrageously high: we will definitely do something about it. The rejection slip from the Op-Ed page of the *Times* of my fine piece "Is a Pigeon Really a Bird, Is an Old Lady Really a Person?," the note from Citibank positive still that the forty-dollar check in question is not a forgery, as I claim, but my own signature, and the alumnae survey from the 1928 class of a small New England junior college are put aside for my private perusal. To Sister I read short notes from Sue, our Texas sister (she's feeling much better, hardly misses the two breasts at all), Ross, our vitamin cousin from Beaumont (he's sending rose hips), Sherry, the child we help support in a rural southern school (her class is going on a bus tour to Washington: could we suggest how she could raise money for the trip?), Luke, our cornball correspondent down in Jack Daniel's country (the poke sallet is ripe, folks), then show her the folder from the American Library Association. She perks up. Though pretending the reverse, she loves a convention, with its lure of the road, busy meetings, and cocktail parties, and in her heyday went to any even slightly within her wide scope of interests. Frequently she was asked to chair. She came to the point, knew her Robert's Rules, and cut down the gabbers.

"I'm glad that's all over," she says now. "I've been bored to death at my last convention, thank goodness."

I try glad tidings from the Cathedral of St. John the Divine. For the building program (a tower or two are missing) it's selling stone, cut, numbered, boasted, and signed in its own traditional stoneyard on the Cathedral grounds.

"For $100 you will receive an elegant certificate which identifies your individually numbered ashlar."

She does not wish her ashlar numbered and identified, or her name inscribed in the Golden Book of Remembrance, and begins to bob. George, her beau, said he had first noticed something was wrong with Sister when they would go out to dinner and her head would bob into the chicken Tetrazzini before she drank her wine even. "Sister," I say, and to get her attention read her the letter from my twelve-year-old Nigerian Pen Pal, inherited from a former Peace Corps friend who had promised to find, but could not, a male correspondent of his own age. Nor could I find one, but in our correspondence, contrived, and full of potential pratfalls on my end, have led him to believe I am Hank James, a boy approximately his age, with literary and athletic ambitions and living with an old aunt in whose care he addresses the letters.

" 'Dear Hank,' " I read aloud. " 'That must have been some ball game, 8–2, with 16 strikeouts. I didn't realize you were the pitcher for the Yankees. Over here we have not so much baseball as soccer which my cousins and I play. When I come to your country I will show you how. Please send me newspaper pictures of you in your Yankee uniform. Also try to come to the point more in your letters. I have showed some to Mr. Akabu, my essay writing teacher, who says you display some talent for a boy your age, but we have a saying here Don't walk a mile to go around the block to see your neighbor who lives next door.

" 'Thanks for the record of the Rolling Stones. I'm glad you like the one I sent.

" 'News here is scarce and petrol is high. Though our country is very high in production, it is very interested in conserving it. It has rained here for several days and we don't go out, that way we save petrol. How much petrol does your Honda use?

" 'By the way, how big is your penis? Please measure it and let me know about this and what is regulation size in your country? Your pal, Geoffrey.' "

The head of the reference librarian is no longer bobbing. "Does he mean girth or overall length?"

"He doesn't specify."

"Then it's not a well-presented question." she says. "We once had a similar one from a man in New Jersey regarding his son. Or himself, I suspect. Anyway, we looked for the answer. There are no reference tools on the subject per se but sometimes in body structure texts there's a mention, though not demographic or by countries. There's absolutely nothing in Survey Graphic or Who's Who and certainly not in Poets and Writers, Bartlett's Quotations, or Moody's Industrials. We finally got a probable answer from a page boy of the same age. Stripped right there in the stacks. He didn't have his proper working permit, so had to submit. Never came back to work, though."

This sick old woman, a great tease in one of her bright moments when the blood is flowing right, rattles her glass and would like to shock me. Is she kidding now? I can't tell but hope she is and am kind of afraid she isn't. I work on our drinks and give her a good dollop, deserved, in her glass. "Two and a half inches. But you must check with a later edition," she says. "This was some time ago and we did it in centimeters."

I do not read her the two P.S.'s: "1. How is the old queer, your tante? 2. We are having a contest in school. There is a strong possibility I may win a trip to your city soon."

The phone rings. It is five forty-five. George, Sister's hearty beau from the nursing home in the Bronx, calls on schedule, after his supper and before the news and sports. They had seemed natural mates—she of West 112th Street, he of East 112th—but his totally unexpected marriage, while drunk, to one who would not divorce him has kept their thirty-five-year romance platonic but alive. Platonic as far as I know, of course. Though on a pay telephone with limited time, after a request of me—will I please buy him another right-handed glove; the one he uses to pull the wheelchair is ripping—he asks, "How're the cats?" "They're right here. Can't you hear them?" and I go "Meow." It's foolish but it amuses the cats, and George, who wants to be fooled, laughs while he waits for Sister to slant on her walker to the phone. The only person she bothers to answer, he calls her darling and asks if she's had her drink and how does she feel? He never dwells on his own troubles—the loneliness and lack of privacy, a roommate who spits on the floor, attendants who steal his telephone dimes. He talks a lot about food; the portions are getting smaller but are still tasty, the pie infinitesimal but delicious. After her exaggeratedly cordial "Hel-lo-o" all Sister says is, "I can't hear, I can't hear." Except that he is alone and needs a touch of the outside world, one wonders why he bothers to spend the daily dime. An old snapshot of Sister in her middy blouse and basketball bloomers, her hair puffed over her ears, her front teeth protruding through a deceptively shy smile, stays in his wallet.

I, a volunteer next-of-kin to several, am listed as his, and now help Sister put the receiver back on the hook. The student soprano upstairs is practicing and I go to our street window directly below hers to shut out the noise. She has a new way of getting her voice out, apparently very painful. Her coach read it in an old Italian book. When I lift the screen to pull down the window the cats leap over the cluster of plants beneath it—wandering Jews, prayer plants, ferns full of self-doubt, a palm tree in a large utility pot that Evelyn uses for a bathroom and Sister to stub out her cigarettes—orphans of the basement growing over the graves of little birds.

As the cats jump to the windowsill I hold them close for fear they'll climb to the narrow railing. Martha bucks and I let them down to the floor of the miniature balcony. We have our last look for the day.

Down the street the rose windows of the Cathedral catch the low rays of the sun. It's a sight. The cats kiss each other and stick their heads through the railings to see better. Across the street Mrs. Ordway, leaning on her window pillow with her big cat, waves at them. Mrs. Harkness comes down the street, giving Ronny, her Scottie, his late afternoon stroll past the ginkgo trees. She walks slowly, shuffling a little, stopping every step or two to breathe heavily, as she did in the hall. Ronny sets his pace to hers; now and then he looks up at her. Mrs. Ordway waves at them, points up, and Mrs. Harkness waves at me and the cats. In the eaves of the Christian Science Church pigeons are kissing. I observe that pigeons rarely wave, even on narrow ledges, but kiss almost more than anybody, except young couples who all but mount on the street. Pigeons and cats and young people kissing—what's in it for old ladies except waving and the old-lady kiss?

Mugging, that's what. Don't you know that somebody across the street watches you every time you bring those cats to the window? They've got those high-powered binoculars that can see anything. Don't you know that Mrs. Ordway with all that big waving is just a decoy, and that she traps and eats all those doves and finches you fatten on sunflower seed?

The soprano hits a high, bad note, the kids on the street hoot, and the cats look up, offended. I let down the window and we return to the living room. Sister is talking back to the TV. "Oven-ready chickens, my eye. When's any self-respecting chicken ever ready for the oven?"

I roll out the depleted bar, unfold the TV tables, and on a mixture of good china and oleo ware we have our supper —okra, meal, and ham in a dish which many may know as coo-coo but which we call "Old Cole" after a Negro man who worked for my grandfather, broiled shrimps stolen from cats, chitlins with a relish made of bean sprouts that our friends the Huangs keep under the bed, smothered lettuce (a ruse Southerners use to get their greens and their grease), and smashed persimmon and whipped cream. By inclination no devotees of the health/organic school, we do not go in much for old-lady food, either. I, a wishful vegetarian, fare well and cheat often on the shameless excuse that *Sister* must have "proper" food. Raised on quinine, calomel, paregoric, and my grandfather's Worcestershire sauce, we have strong stomachs and, some say, weak brains.

Martha stands in front of me, watching me eat. I spare her a chitlin on a paper napkin, she hisses at it and prisses over to the fireplace, where she tries to dislodge the impedimenta put there to keep her from climbing the chimney. The first night with us she went up the chimney, came down on the other side in our neighbor Jenny's apartment, and ate all her spider plants and a design for I. M. Pei. The sidesaddle slips; tiny, it had belonged to my mother, an equestrienne of renown who had fallen off it in a UDC parade and broken both arms. But the huge Books in Print holds. To hide her defeat Martha stands still and cocks her ears as though she hears someone in the hall. On to her tricks (*I* don't hear anything), I eat her chitlin. The intercom, believed broken, rings. "Who is it?" A falsetto voice answers me: "To be or not to be. Open up and see." Street kids playing a joke. We hope.

We turn on the early TV news and watch a handicapped child get ready to go to school. He crawls to the couch and holds on. Kneeling, his mother hitches on his braces, and the car comes. She puts him in the car and they kiss. He has two hearing aids and cerebral palsy.

White, with no notes or identification, the body of a

baby is found in the garbage can outside a school. A slain policeman, ten years on the force, is buried while his widow and four children watch. An old lady is raped in the hall of her project apartment and her throat slit; we see the covered body. A young man is stabbed trying to help an elderly man who's being mugged. A young woman has her baby in the trying-on room for Misses Dresses of a big department store. Holding them over her stomach, she carries three dresses past the checker, pulls the curtains of the small room, hangs up the dresses neatly, and gives birth. She had no other private place. Three children die in a fire. Their father has just brought two to safety outside the burning house and goes to find the other. The two rush back into the house looking for their dog. How do people whose three children die in a fire face any moment of any day ever? Surely they have a greater belief, or disbelief, than I.

It is rumored that the father set the fire.

Two shaken old women, we switch stations and watch old Walter cronk it out, then switch again and pretend to listen to a Wall Street report. Nothing else on tonight's program interests us and we both yawn, anxious to go to our rooms—Sister to be alone and think, or snore, or wonder what happened to her, and me likewise, but also to fight for bed rights, and read. Sister no longer reads, though she holds Proust in front of her for a long time, or a life of Lady Bird Johnson, whom she admires. Before we part we swap choice idiocies of the day—a gem she had heard on a soap opera: "Sometimes it is necessary to resort to a lie to hide the truth"; and a graffito I'd seen on the park wall: "Pollution is terrible. Suck my dick." (Had one of the playground children written it? Was that why the little boy was smiling so? Nonsense, he couldn't have spelled pollution.) We do not edit, nor ever have edited, raw contributions. Sister, a lifetime librarian and longtime supporter of ACLU and Roger Baldwin, does not believe in censorship.

"Environmental concern" is her comment now, and we rise to go to our rooms. Sister, sick and older, with the higher social security check, has the larger bedroom. I watch her creak down the hall toward it on her walker. Her latest stroke was in July, and she is still determined to dress and bathe herself. "Anybody could have written it," she says, and when she closes her door I proceed to the kitchen for the night fight.

6

Defeat is the name of the roach game. Even though I sometimes seem to win I always know that I have lost. Combat is risky, slippery work, totally ineffective if the exterminator has recently been with his supply of vitamins, and killing anything except cancer-related cells is not high on my list of the sporting. Immunized to all the tried toxic preparations, my adversaries succumb only to bodily blows. By using the Pittsburgh pitcher throw, and firing one of Cousin Ross's health food tablets, I can, if lucky, stun a roach at three feet, then finish him off—maybe—with my shoe. Or, as another fine pitcher said, "If I can throw that way [good] consistently, in games, guys won't be able to sit back and watch for the fast ball."

My targets, as deft in dodging the pellets as Sister is the old-lady kiss, quickly encircle me, *Swan Lake*–ing and pointy-toeing, and render my sidewinder useless. After the scheduled ten minutes of hit and miss, Rupert (fairy, my eye), busy watching the young girls skitter across the linoleum on their sexy young legs, steps forward, like the senior reporter at press conferences, to signal the end of the contest of wits. Bowing to his seniority, the other roaches scatter, we all agree it's a pretty futile exercise (but the cats enjoy it), promise to meet on the morrow, and I tie up the garbage and hasten back to the Oval Office.

Tonight it does not happen this way. Impatient with the old priority, Lester, a newcomer, one of the fiery young what's-in-it-for-me? breed, confronts Rupert. What are my rights? He stands in front of Rupert, demanding. I'm entitled. Rupert stares him down and walks with dignity toward his office under the sink. But Rupert is on the skids. Lester is now our crack anchor man. This is very disturbing, I think, and give them both the sole of my shoe. So much for male roaches with first names.

Admiring the hanging beauties across the court, the cats and I water the scroungy little step-plants Margarita has found to spruce up our kitchen window. Upstairs Eddie Fuller, the combo player, is tooting his goodnight horn, and we listen, hoping for "At the Devil's Ball," or at the very least "Chloe," still asked for at the anniversaries by the more ancient who, like the cats and me, just love that long, lingering wail way out there in the dreary swampland. "Chlo——eee." But we get the same old soaked coins in the fountain, and I drag the big black garbage bag to the front, where the cats have their nocturnal fling down the hall. Martha tries for a visit, but I guard the stairs. The elevator passes our floor, no one on it. It goes on to the eighth and comes back still with no visible passengers. It'll probably be stuck in the morning. I hurry the cats inside, lock our three locks, and in moving the small desk with the undelivered packages knock off the one for the Mad Scientist. Secured against attackers from the elevator—at least we'll hear the package fall (did it actually squeal or was that eerie little cry the door hinge squeaking? Was it "Chloe"?)—we come back to the room we "share."

The light switch is a string hung from the ceiling. Evelyn stands on the dresser, jumps, and pulls on the light. (Why is your electric bill so high? I'll tell you why—it's that cat.) "The last one in is a rotten egg," I say, and from the best place on the bed they watch me. With a reluctant glance in the mirror I see me as I must appear to them—a scrawny-faced, long-nosed, loose-necked, turkey-wattled, big-butted, half-pleasant old woman who's stopped using lipstick but still cuts her own hair (what's left of it), who's quit snapping her beans but still likes her beer cold, an old lady clinging to an outmoded notion of fair play, flinging herself on the bed trying to get her share.

Bested, I get up and sprinkle the sunflower seed on the windowsill for our morning visitors. Across the street Mrs. Ordway watches me fasten the screen (I do not get my kicks setting up birds for cats) and waves her big leaf. I curb my natural instinct to tell her in what nice cozy nook to put it for the night, rest on the end of the pillow Martha allows me, find my bifocals under the bed where the cats, playing scat, have accidentally(?) knocked them with my notebook, and lie down with my nightly can of beer. Opening the new book of Whitman, I choose at random from *Song of the Open Road.*

"Do you know what it is as you pass to be loved by strangers? Do you know the talk of those turning eyeballs?" Somebody (Cookie Rothberg?) has written in the border "Who was his oculist? Or was he talking about a horse?"

When I was born, Sister, six years my senior and in no mood for baby-sitting, had hoped *I* would be a horse, not the ordinary Shetland pony mild-mannered children want, and so easy on my recently widowed mother, but one of those broad-backed, knot-tailed Rosa Bonheur types she'd seen in the Art and Literature Reader. Queen of the Horse Fair, she had fancied something she could stand on, circus style, with her golden hair reflected in the sparkling waters of Sandy Creek as she splashed through reciting "Cromwell, I charge thee, fling away ambition" or "Milton! thou shouldst be living at this hour," quotables she had lifted secondhand from my mother. And on the other side of the foaming creek, two feet deep, Chuck Paramore, sixteen, shot-putter and extemporaneous debater, would snatch at the flying mane (of the horse) and claim her for his own just as she finished off with "Sail on, sail on, O Ship of State!" He in turn would tear into the affirmative side of "Should the government control the railroads?" or perhaps, wordless with longing, ravish her on the spot—after she got off the horse, a large unfriendly Percheron without bridle and named Diable.

With dramatic urges such as these, it seemed natural that Sister be allowed further histrionic pursuit, especially since she was independently wealthy. As children we all made our spending money as best we could—picking or shelling the little field peas for our grandfather, selling medicine bottles and old trusses back to the drugstore, sweeping with brush brooms the hard dirt of the extensive backyard, feeding the chickens or knocking the roosters off the hens (we were told they were fighting), or, behind my grandmother's back, sneaking bourbon into my grandfather's iced tea. My grandfather, a retired general store merchant, paid the going slave wages—fifty cents a day for pea pickers, two cents a rooster, a dime a shot for the iced tea. With scant book learning of his own, he was proud of our records at school and free with the silver dollar awards for outstanding feats. Fragile, fiery, almost fiercely bright, Sister had made her roll, not as a field hand or rooster knocker, but by skipping grades and spelling deceptive words in county and district contests—privilege, prophesy, kimono.

In 1910 she had six dollars, and after breezing through the after-school chores my grandmother, a former Latin teacher, gave her—conjugating three new Latin verbs and refreshing the water in the Rhode Island Red receptacles on which Sister pasted the warning "Bibi a su Periculum," which my grandmother removed and pasted back, corrected—she was permitted to cross the road and take elocution lessons at twenty-five cents a throw from our neighbor, Miss Roxie Redlake.

"Throw" is used advisedly. A nurse and what we would now call physical therapist, Miss Roxie had come to town a stranger, the second wife of our tubercular friend Mr. C.T., who had fallen for her strong ways in the Beaumont Hospital and whom, by overexercising, people said, she had contrived to outlive. His holdings had been of some worth and Miss Roxie became by inheritance and sheer sinew a prominent member of the community. After Mr. C.T.'s death she had torn down his chicken house, razed his mule lot, mowed over his turnip patch fronting the school yard, and built the first and finest croquet court in town.

Now, we were not country bumpkins. Though not of the city as was Miss Roxie, we were not from Doodledy Squat either. We had played croquet and had even heard of golf. Anybody who lives in the country can pick up a tree limb (small one), knock a pine burr or a cow cake down the lane, and call it hockey, golf, or croquet. Nor were we ignorant of tennis. In one of his shipments Mr. Percy, my grandfather's wholesale contact in Galveston, had included a damaged net, and we soon learned to paddle balls over it and "ace it" through the big hole. Sue even developed an eccentric little backhand. But we did it for fun. We never laid out courts and measured distances. We just set up a net or a wicket or two somewhere after we'd eaten supper, and whacked a few. We kind of made it a pleasure. Not Miss Roxie. Something was going rat-tat-a-tat in Miss Roxie's blood that said "Nix on the pleasure. Make it a business. Be first." And in a way I think this same force was beating in Sister, too, but it was going for the brain and not for the body. That she and Miss Roxie finally clashed was not too unexpected.

Miss Roxie organized the Five Towns Croquet Club

and, using the risqué pendulum shot (between her legs), became not only county champion but Leader of our local imitation Camp Fire Girls group. Then, like the mouse, she began to overreach. She aspired to become a sort of intellectual arbiter and "gave" lessons in dramatic readings, emphasizing breath control and body movement. Though a bit ampullaceous, she was a fine-looking woman, large without being fat, and where the neck of the bottle met the more ample spread below, where the juicy part was, she was truly handsome. Having had rickets as a child, she had built up her own bones and muscles from scratch. Somewhere along the comeback trail she had dabbled in reading/speaking and, through a radical Methodist fringe of a YWCA outing, had come in contact with a copy of *Leaves of Grass*. Impressed with his glorification of the body, she from then on assigned her pupils, along with "Work, work, work," "Row, row, row," "Tramp, tramp, tramp," and similar muscular exhortations, selections from the outdoor Whitman.

Sister, schooled in the more orthodox rhythms of the English Lake and Latin poets, fell for the Good Gray as enthusiastically as she had for Chuck Paramore. This enthusiasm brought out a wild, flamboyant side of her that at times threatened to burst her frail frame, and that seemed totally incongruous with the down-to-earth side of one whose frequent observation was already "This is ridiculous," and whose forty-year diary came to consist almost wholly of a day-by-day account of expenditures for gas and cigarettes (gas—6 gallons for $1.05 in 1944, cigarettes 18 cents a pack).

Why she was so smitten has never been clear, except that Whitman by "arousing" all those "unanswerable questions" (his own brag) may have awakened her considerable interest in research. "Is it not something that has been better told and done before?" Which "it"? Before what? "Does it answer universal needs?" What "universe" do you have in mind? Define "needs." "What blurt is this about virtue and about vice?" *Whose* "virtue," *whose* "vice"? I think that Sister, destined, as we have seen, to do some of her rarest work answering unconventional questions at the reference desk, may have sensed an early ally and challenge. She would never say—if she knew.

The friction that grew between her and Miss Roxie was that of opposites. Miss Roxie's strength was in the physical, the muscular, the exercise of the body, and a beautiful thing to see, too, on the croquet grounds or in her Camp Fire Leader knickers. Her eye-fringes, iris, upper-arms, armpits, elbow-sockets, ribs, belly, backbone, joints of the backbone, appeared to be just as superb as her mentor Whitman espoused. Her embouchures were in crackerjack order, and her arrogance was that of the formidable self-made. Literary perhaps she was, but only in the way that a fullback is. I now recognize that she was before her time, a Mary Wigman of the hinterlands. The low-slung grief, the floor grovel, the flailing backlash, the walking squat, the unuttered howl, the tortured torso, the joyous embrace of earth and air—all were present in Miss Roxie's Whitman.

Sister, who since the age of three had been reading, often two books at a time, and could divide all Gaul as expertly as my grandmother, found her strength in the cerebral. But each seemed to be unconsciously, or consciously, trying to enter the other's domain. Sister would stagger home from a lesson with Miss Roxie pale and goggle-eyed from exertion, and my mother would rub her body with honeysuckle lotion. Peering through the branches of the crape myrtle and between the grazing cows on the roadside, we could see Miss Roxie lying in the porch hammock, book in hand, slowly turning the pages, or not turning them at all. Was she on the next assignment or the past one? How far back was she? Now and then she would dash out to the croquet court, grab a mallet, and, taking aim, knock a roqueted ball over the gully to the school yard. And Sister would hold on to her head, as if to make sure it was not rolling out of bounds toward the flagpole.

But Miss Roxie, no piker, would soon be back in the hammock, worrying the pages again, trying to keep up. Assigned *one* page, Sister would learn *ten,* and Miss Roxie would then have to read ten, too, in order to prepare the appropriate gestures and breathing. Whether Sister acted with ill intent, or because she could not slow her grasp to conform to Miss Roxie's limited reach, I never knew. I do know that often I felt sorry for Miss Roxie, who looked lonely and not all that built up out there in the hammock, bent over the book.

Only Sister, I imagine, was more lonely. Resented by those she skipped over, shunned by those she skipped to, too proud to settle for the company of her younger kin, she led a solitary life except for the Rhode Island Reds and her books. But Miss Roxie was not only lonely, she was lost, with Sister three lessons ahead of her always, and with both of them knowing that she (Miss Roxie) would never catch up with her. "Slow down a little, Sister," suggested my mother, a compassionate onlooker. "You're killing Miss Roxie."

But Miss Roxie asked no quarter and gave none. She went up from twenty-five to thirty-five cents on her lessons; Sister skipped another grade, our grandfather forked over another dollar, and the contest continued. Peeping at them through the crape myrtle, I thought they were equally great, and I, too, became a Whitman fan. On one rare occasion when Sister allowed me (my mother made her) to accompany her to her lesson, I listened to Miss Roxie and, overcoming a childish impulse to giggle hysterically at any performance slightly outré (most revivals and all high singers) became convinced forever. Advancing from behind the porch hammock as though from some proud proscenium, Miss Roxie reached center stage and, looking down at me, front-row seated on the top steps, gave a star-studded rendition of "the one" people said "she'd got" Mr. C.T. with:

"Smile O voluptuous cool-breath'd earth!
Earth of the slumbering and liquid trees!
Earth of departed sunset—earth of the mountains misty-topt!
Earth of the vitreous pour of the full moon just tinged with blue!
Earth of shine and dark mottling the tide of the river!
Earth of the limpid gray of clouds brighter and clearer for my sake!
Far-swooping elbow'd earth—rich apple-blossom'd earth!
Smile, for your lover comes."

Looking up at her from the steps, as Mr. C.T., laid low in Beaumont, must have looked up at her as she came nearer and nearer to the hospital bed, I understood why he had not been able to, or even tried to, resist her. Missing his mules and his turnip patch, homesick for pastures where his chickens grazed, he had been fair game for earth conjure. Though aware that this was not the ordinary TB cure, that Miss Roxie was courting his money, not his wilted old body (plenty told him so), sure that his family would fight it, and that out there in the real periculum he would lose, he had at the same time, through Miss Roxie and Whitman, felt that *he* was the earth.

At least, that's the way I sure felt when, smiling, just exactly like my lover, Miss Roxie came toward me on the top steps. And though I had pulled back a little where Mr. C.T. had not, it seemed to me that Miss Roxie had won the contest between her and Sister hands down. But later at home, listening with the Rhode Island Reds to Sister practicing under the house, I wavered.

"The sun and stars that float in the open air,
The apple-shaped earth and we upon it, surely the drift of them is something grand . . ."

Cackling their applause, the hens drowned out Sister for a few lines and then she broke in again:

"The endless pride and outstretching of man, unspeakable joys and sorrows,
The wonder every one sees in every one else he sees, and the wonders that fill each minute of time forever,
What have you reckon'd them for, camerado?"

Singling out a noisy old hen, Sister looked at her intently. Caught cackling, camerado looked up at me, and together we lowered our eyes and reckoned it was still a mighty close race.

Things came to a head between Miss Roxie and Sister one June. "What is the grass?" Sister asked a camping group on the banks of the Angelina River near our East Texas home. No bona fide affiliate of any known organization, this was, rather, a bucolic offshoot of Miss Roxie's imagination, doing it its own way in bloomers, middy blouses, bare feet, and mail-order cowgirl suits from Bellas Hess and National Cloak Suit Company. Its members bore small, if any, resemblance to the Camp Fire Girls we followed so avidly *In the Maine Woods*, *On Sunrise Hill*, and *On the Open Road*, the last a real bummer that turned out to be not on the Open Road at all in the free, laissez-faire sense we had come to expect from Whitman's Road, but in a dumpy little town in Arkansas where they said "whar" and nobody had "the experience"—a clear-cut explanation of which, instead of fine talk and girlish pledges, we were all looking for.

Of college age (physically), these fictional paragons glorified work, sought beauty, gave service, pursued knowledge, held on to health, tied knots, excelled in bead work and bold basketry, said "Daggers and dirks" when they cursed, sang "Marching Through Georgia" as a hiking song, were named Chapa the Chipmunk and Sahwah the Sun Fish, suffered from mal de raquette, which had nothing to do with the bad tennis we played through the hole in Mr. Percy's net, had a hymn about the Hidden Fire and the Sheltering Flame—and could hardly strike a match without setting something on fire. Look around and the cheesecloth was blazing. Few were Marxists.

But boy, could they identify nature!

Not so Sister, who spent her leisure time under the back steps reading, not matching up leaves or throwing pine cones in the woods.

"What is the grass?" Sister held out her hands in her elocution gesture for grass, turned on her body culture voice, and let loose what she and Whitman both must have considered a showstopper. "Is this the handkerchief of the Lord?"

Miss Roxie, hot-tempered and haggard, backed away from her. "No, and it's not the beautiful uncut hair of graves, either. Or the colorless beards of old men."

Miss Roxie had had Sister for three months now. Her croquet aim was off, her elbow sockets were shot, she was loose in the knees, and Mr. C.T.'s family was contesting the will. Sister, on the other hand, on both hands, in fact, was growing stronger. Her arm muscles were so developed she could outchin any challengers (except my sister Sue), her fingers so limber no one in recital could rondo through Alla Turca as fast (except Mozart and my sister Sue), and, wrestling, she could hold all comers' shoulders to the ground (except my sister Sue's). Her breath control now enabled her to stay underwater longer than anybody else in Sandy Creek (except Chuck Paramore—and my sister Sue). None of the Whitman exercises had unbowed her legs or lessened her lisp (playing dirty, Miss Roxie, to demean her, assigned "No dainty dolce affettuoso I"), but she had skipped another grade by this time, spelled "pyrrhuloxia" in the district meet, picked a peck of field peas, bought her own copy of Whitman, and was going to Miss Roxie for extra sessions.

Holding the weed out beseechingly, she advanced on the Leader. "What *is* the grass?" This time Miss Roxie yelled. "It's poison ivy, you little show-out pismire. I'll wrap the handkerchief of the Lord around you. And don't you ever come near me again, you bowlegged, snot-nosed, grade-skipping little shit."

This was not de rigueur Camp Fire language, but Miss Roxie was really, or so said my mother, looking at Sister sideways, "not to blame."

Sister, maybe, at that time couldn't tell one leaf from another unless it was big as an oak or in a book; many could roll a poncho or a Bull Durham neater; some could whistle a truer but not louder tune through their fists or their fore- and little fingers; a few could chant with as much feeling as Sister the local substitute for the real Camp Fire Girls' Work, Health, Love incantations: "Cabeza de vaca, Head of a cow, Pull down your pants, I'll show you how." None could come quicker or straighter to the point of a matter as she. "Finito," she announced of her association with Miss Roxie. But the two were to tangle twice more.

When the poison ivy sores were healed (Sister's, because

of her superior physical condition, much quicker than those of Miss Roxie, who was run-down and showing it in her roquets) Sister pursued her own training. Freed of the shackling limitations of Miss Roxie, who now abandoned the literary life to rebuild her long-shot aim, she committed to memory ("to murder," said the skeptical) whole sections of Whitman and to this day is the only person I know, besides Miss Roxie, who ever tackled him with all-out gestures.

Too bright to be doing what she was doing, and no match for Miss Roxie and her more mature interpretations, Sister often went in for the comic. The *Songs* were her favorites and from most she had her standby lines and gestures:

of Myself—"The handkerchief of the Lord" bit (easy, just poke your imaginary handkerchief out in front of you and paw at the tatting trimming).

of the Broad-Axe:
(*Whom have you slaughter'd lately European headsman?*
Whose is that blood upon you so wet and sticky?)
(Stand back, outraged, a safe distance from the axe, and make the cut sign across the throat.)

of the Redwood-Tree:
Farewell my brethren,
Farewell O earth and sky, farewell ye neighboring waters,
My time has ended, my term has come.
(Spread your hands out like farewell, or a preacher passing the collection plate, then fall down—*Timber!*)

of Joys:
O ripen'd joy of womanhood! O happiness at last!
I am more than eighty years of age . . .
How clear is my mind—how all people draw nigh to me!

(Imitate people getting as far as possible from the old woman.)

of the Answerer:
He says indifferently and alike How are you friend? *to the President at his levee,*
And he says Good-day my brother, *to Cudge that hoes in the sugar-field,*
And both understand him and know that his speech is right.
(Leave this one alone, or do it straight-faced.)

But these were all mere come-ons, curtain raisers. Except for the turning eye-balls motif in *Song of Myself*, it was always *Song for Occupations*, rich in interpretative material, that was the core of her act. After several full pages of philosophical excursion, the poem gets down to facts and lists up to sixty-six occupations with offshoot references to the tools, working conditions, and questionable joys of steady employment (Workman! . . . your daily life!). Starting with house-building, measuring, sawing the boards, blacksmithing, glass-blowing, nail-making, coopering, tin-roofing, shingle-dressing, Sister did not shirk a single profession. Shifting from one to another with a muscular diversity that fairly exhausted her and her faithful audience (me, my mother, my grandmother, and the Rhode Island Reds), she became endowed with phenomenal breathing control which cleared up a worrisome little nasal drip that had led Miss Roxie to call her snot-nosed, and which gave her rare discipline in time of stress.

In 1914, when the first airplane most of us had ever seen had flown over the schoolhouse, Sister (ten now, me four, Sue six, Brother eight) had not run screaming into the school yard like the rest of her classmates and teachers, convinced the Germans had come. Instead she arranged her ribbon rosettes over her ears, anchored her middy blouse on her belly button, blew through her teeth straighteners, wet her fingers to set the pleats in her skirt, and walked resolutely to the front of the building, where she positioned herself on the top step. Assuming her customary stance by the flagpole—a long-jointed unstable cane out of Miss Blanche Cunningham's Aubusson carpet from St. Louis, and somewhat like the cane pole our sister Sue later taught us to use in pole vaulting—she saluted. Calmed by her bravery, we stopped running and screaming and followed suit.

Across the red clay road, in Miss Roxie's championship grounds, the County Croquet Club was having its annual competition. Ladies from Buna, Kirbyville, and as far away as Silsbee had put on their gingham sunbonnets, and their divided skirts that would not impede the advantageous pendulum swing, and come for the kill. Miss Roxie, who hadn't won her county championship by daintsy-dipping like September morn around the wickets (vanquished adversaries claimed her mallet loaded, her wickets magnetized, and her balls nonregulation), was out for her third straight championship. She did not intend to permit any outside disturbance from either Sister or the airplane. Watching from center wicket, she raised a warning mallet at both.

The plane seemed to falter but Sister stood firm. "Allons, Camerados," she cried and, swiftly breaking into "Turning eye-balls" as a crowd soother, switched and ripped into *Song for Occupations*. The plane kept circling the school yard, coming lower and lower. Now we could see the man in the cockpit (we learned the term later), a murderous-looking Hun. He shouted and waved something in his arms threateningly—was that a Belgian baby he was about to dash to death? Sister kept on with her occupations; we kept saluting. Every time she would take on a new trade—ship-joining, dock-building, fish-curing, flagging of sidewalks by flaggers—Sister would turn her eye-balls toward the low-circling plane and grab the flag-pole. She quit only when the plane, off course to the Annual Fair in Beaumont, ran out of gas and the terrified pilot, waving a "Help, help" sign, made a forced landing on the croquet grounds just as Miss Roxie bent her elbows a wily way she had in contests (they also said she was a morphadite), took aim, made one of her long jump shots, and knocked the flagpole down.

The cats move, restless, and we go in for a last check on Sister. She is lying quietly in bed, eyes closed. She is breathing. Is she thinking—of what? Death, what does Aix mean, Disraeli, Chuck Paramore, George in the nursing home, the horror-stricken page boy in the stacks, the frantic pilot in the cockpit, whatever? Or is she asleep? She doesn't speak and we go back to "our" room, leaving the door ajar so we can hear her.

Standing on her hind legs, Evelyn jumps, catches the string, and pulls out the light (Yes, but she can turn them *off*, too). The streetlight streams through the slits where the shade skimps, and plays on the ceiling. I lie and watch it, worried: had she really been breathing? Why was she lying so still, stricken and helpless, her hand outstretched, fingers raised as though summoning aid? Or was it a warmed-over Whitman gesture, the "What is the grass?" come-on? Chasing a star-shaped wedge of light, Evelyn leaps from my stomach and clings by her toenails to the wall molding, six feet above the bed. Martha watches, amused, daring me to leave her dangling there for the night; we would have more room. Evelyn disengages herself and drops back on top of us. I get up and hang a sheet over the light spot. The door opens wider. Sister is there, awake, her hand still outstretched.

"Okay, Hank the Yank, hop on your Honda and hand me my cigarettes you're hiding from me in that dirty bag with that diseased dead bird."

When she has gone, I open, by light coming through the sheet, my notebook, not so much a journal as a sort of loose-leaf catchall of childhood memories, senile non sequiturs, salient facts, location of recipes and clippings—a hodgepodge it seemed relevant to start recording when it became evident that Sister wasn't the only one losing her memory. "Remember to tell Sister about the man picking up the children's books at the stall," I write. "Why did he look back at me as if he knew who I was?

"Never tell her of the appointment notice."

No need to; she is back at the door and tells *me*. "I do not mean extinct things of which there is none. I mean things which claim they are the only one. I'm talking about Robin Redbreast. And if you have five months and three weeks before you're due for your next mugging, why do you keep getting those appointment notices under the door?"

7

At two-thirty the phone rings and Ray, the renovated rooster, calls, drunk, from Miami. One of his cats, Girl Baby, has peed on his summa cum laude and it's turned red (from Harvard, it was in a crimson folder). I sympathize, but barely, and while he goes to get another beer, hang up and take an aspirin. At six o'clock the doves from the Christian Science Church whir onto the windowsill, my bedmates lunge across me at the screen, I register what day of the week it is, who's dead, who's not, turn off the transistor (batteries gone again), and the day begins.

The pigeons, drumming and devouring ("Sure some of them are drumming and devouring, like other friends of mine"), follow the doves, and at six-thirty the redheaded house finches, singing lovely little arias, bring whole families to breakfast. I replenish the supply of sunflower seed and they eat, splitting and flipping the seeds with their sharp bills, then, having pecked the sill bare, line up for aerial gymnastics on a loose antenna wire. The females are gray, with white stripes, plain, but thought none the less for it by either the cats or the brightly colored male finches, and are as good or better on the high wire and the high notes than their mates. Watching the tiny bobbing heads, the cats cry and pounce. The screen holds but the sheet/shade falters. I prop it with a piece of wood.

At seven the cats can tolerate it no longer and shove me toward the kitchen. We look in Sister's room. She is breathing but not stirring. The bathroom door is open and the cats push past me. The mouse is gone and all present know no cat, however gifted with lights, has lifted the container lid and freed him. Evelyn sets herself under the bathtub faucet for her morning meditation on water—where does it come from? What is the true source? If three fourths of the earth is covered with it, why is this drip so small?

Because there's no heat or hot water again, dear, I explain, and in the kitchen find the pilot light out (a roach did it) and light the gas with a match. A small fire ensues, but no damage except to the potholder, too slow in getting out of the way, and I put on the coffee and open a can of Dixie Dinner, promptly covered with a dish towel by my friends, who run up the stepladder to pose for pictures. At the front door I pick up the paper, surprised as always to find it really there, the locks, desk, and packages, too, for that matter. The cats are gourmandizing on cobwebs inside the china closet, which they unlatch and enter at will, and the bed is all mine at last.

I pour a cup of coffee and spread out the paper. What old- or young-timers have bit the obit dust today? What food places have been cited for violations (rats in the pantry)? What other sparkling essay, brimming with living quotes ("Sure it's fun to be recognized by a pigeon or a jaybird") has not been printed on the Op-Ed page? Before I can find out, the phone rings. It's Eddie Fuller. His neighbor, a nurse from St. Luke's Hospital, is stuck in the elevator, stalled on the eighth floor. He has to hurry to work but has called the super for help. Would I go up one flight and just speak to her and let her know somebody is there? He has some country bacon for me.

I put on Something Suitable, grab the coffeepot and two cups, shut the cats in "our" room, and hurry up. She is young and pretty and looks at me through the small round window of the elevator door. "I'm thankful you're here," she says. "I'm sorry you're in *there.*" I hit the door with my fist. The handle does not budge. We look at each other, smiling, and wait for help. "Kick it a little inside," Erich Gottchalck comes out of his apartment and tells her. She kicks, it moves an inch, and, afraid it will fall, she quits. Erich hurries down the steps to hunt super. We keep smiling through the little window. "Can you sit down?" I ask. "I'd rather stand." She is now looking at the sign on the inside door that says *Please Return Cab to Lobby* and is holding tight to the railings inside the cab. Giving me a telephone number, she asks me to tell St. Luke's why she is late. "Will she come to work?" someone in the nursing station asks me. "She'd certainly like to." For God's sake. "She's *stuck.*"

She's still smiling when I take a stool and go back upstairs. Erich comes up the stairs, breathless, says super is on his way, and goes into his apartment to flop. I sit down and try to think of something to say. When I have it I pop up and look in the window. "What does Gabriele mean?" It's her last name and she knows. "It's Italian for Gabriel, the saint." I sit back down, trying to think of something else. She is gazing in the direction of the plaque that records how long it's been since the elevator was inspected (1973). "Your hanging flowers sure are pretty. We can see them from our kitchen window."

"Thank you."

"They're sure prettier than that chewed-up fern of the Huangs."

Now it's her turn.

"How's Martha?"

"Fine. She'll be sorry to miss this. It's a good thing you don't have to go to the bathroom."

She smiles, but weakly. "That's an interesting robe," she says and looks at her watch. It's been forty-five minutes.

"We didn't know it," says the handyman when he rushes down the steps from the roof. "Usually they ring the bell and scream."

"She's not a screamer. Speak to her."

He waves at her through the window and with a wrench undoes a knob at the top of the elevator. The door opens and she walks out. "My legs are weak," she says.

"Sit a minute." I would have to sit for the rest of the day, but she thanks us and walks down the seven flights to work.

Back home with my stool, I check by telephone with Monica, our neighbor—three rings. If she's all right she'll call back—two rings—but I forget when she does and answer. She has to pay after all. We giggle over it—just two more old ladies trying to beat AT&T. She will call *us* tomorrow.

It is now nine o'clock and Margarita comes to clean. She has had to walk up but is still early. "My nose is slipping," she explains. Translation: a nurse for whom she cleans before she comes to us is still sleeping; she did not disturb her. She now regards the sheet in the window. "Putting shits in the window?" "No, taking them out of the window." A fast and feverish worker, she soon finishes the curtain/shade job and, bundling up a pile of old papers from my room, takes them with the laundry ("dirty shits") to the basement.

After Sister has been served breakfast (she blatantly denies letting the mouse go) I fish out the form from the Class of '28. An alumnae survey, it wishes me to check certain boxes: Degrees, Awards, Publications (append extra sheet if necessary), Marriages, Divorces, Anniversaries, Children, Grand, Great. Zeroing in my usual string of inadequacies, I get down to the essay question, kindly included for the few spinsters/nonachievers.

"Using the underscored as guidelines, rate yourself on a scale of 1 to 10 as a success (a) in your profession, (b) as a human being. How much have you changed in the last fifty years? We remember your answers to some of these questions in your 1926 application blank. Do you?"

I'm afraid so. Working backwards, I begin to fill in the blanks.

"Every day you rate differently, every hour even, if you're that self-addicted.

"This goes for *The Person I Most Admire*, too. Today the one I most admire" (Al Smith in 1926. Too early for Mrs. Roosevelt) "is a young nurse in my building, yesterday it was a redheaded down-and-outer who without 'please' or stopping, asked me forthrightly, 'Will you buy me a hot dog? It's fifty cents.' Another day it was the Waver, an old man who waves at people whom he thinks nobody else does, or, in a playful mood, intercepts waves, confusing the unwary, but supplying them with something to think about, often needed. But my admiration is not confined to people. Last night it was a brash young roach, not a type I ordinarily admire, but who alone, and with everything to gain, stepped out of the circle to contest the ruling of the old union boss. Day before yesterday it was a tree I most admired, the day before that part of a conversation overheard on the bus: 'The suburbs, a tree in front, a tree in back, all that quiet, who needs it?'

"Tomorrow who knows? It might even be another old lady.

"*Do I Feel My Life Rich, Fulfilled?* Yes, greatly. I can eat and drink and laugh, watch racehorses in the stretch ('He run real big'), and appreciate a tree anytime. I can be private, and even write a little. More important, I can read.

"Whenever I feel my life getting *un*fulfilled—the frequent fucks of yesteryear gone, all gone, the golden pubic hairs turned to gray, the hit and the miss of winning or losing, the kiss and run, gone, gone—whenever I feel that even the bounty listed above is not all-encompassing—I go to the Home and offer to help those less fortunate than I, buried alive, staring at nothing, or watching their spit or talking to their bowels. Whenever I feel that something is lacking, that that for which I started out so long ago will never be attained, when I cannot even remember what it was I started out for, I read my friends Walt Whitman and Henry James, or Henry James on Walt Whitman. (How wrong could he be!) Or I watch a bird, or buy a book by Cookie Rothberg, or a hat for a cat, or I go to the Cathedral and look at the rose windows. Or I go to the nineteenth-century room at the Met, or simply open my art books at all the Annunciations: Boy, have I got news for you! Guess what?

"Sometimes I just go speak to Kirby.

"What are *My Hopes*, then, besides the no-war, lasting-peace, no-cruelty improbabilities? That the clean livers will always lose out to the drinkers and the smokers, the trainers to the animals, the hunters to the hunted, and all ball clubs to the Mets. That sometime I might have a bed at least two cats wide.

"What things do I consider *Overrated*, besides most public entertainments? Eclipses. Most first editions you can afford. Any fireworks after the first two or three. Tiffany glass of any size, shape, or intention. Falstaff. Woody Allen. Large outsized jazz singers with thousands of dollars and acres of brocade wrapped around them. Scat, and I don't mean cats. Writers writing about how they write.

"*Underrated*. Those who stand up for what they believe even if I don't. Firemen. Women. Men.

"*Pet Peeves*. Bus drivers who give old people with the half-fare card a hard time. Young women who go to scream school to learn how to scream louder (primal). Those glorious Audubon watercolors of stuffed birds—'painted in their natural habitat.' The expressions 'get rid of' (usually means some animal. Contracts a human makes with an animal should be sacred and broken only by consenting sides); 'if something happens to you' (never means anything good); 'given generously of himself' (what *part* of himself? Get definite).

"*Most Interesting Thing I've Done:* Live. *High Point in My Life:* Not marrying and not having children. *Low Point in My Life:* Not marrying and not having children.

"*Ugliest Thing:* Seeing a person or animal mistreated or humiliated by one stronger than they. Seeing the unwanted —children, old parents, pets—cast out, made victims always of others' convenience or whim. *Saddest Thing:* Watching a loved one's hand tremble, seeing the spirit go. *Most Beautiful Thing:* The wit and the wonder and the grace of most animals—and of more people than you'd ever imagine."

I send them fifty bucks, stack my half-baked senilicisms under the bed for scrap paper, and, hedging, answer Pen Pal's inquiry. "Are we not all different? As a great American poet says, 'Because you are greasy or pimpled, or were once drunk, or a thief, / Or that you are diseas'd, or rheumatic . . . / Do you give in that you are any less immortal?' What he means is it's not how big and prominent one is that counts, but what one does for others with the equipment at hand. I think.

"Along with his ball playing, your humble correspondent himself writes, and it is not outside the realm of probability that his letters be collected for posterity. Save any you are fortunate enough to receive, therefore, for the delight and edification of future generations. Also any stories. In progress now is a short story, a gem really, called 'The Pupil,' with the tutor an entirely different character from your Mr. Akabu, who seems a rather sordid, unsavory type. In my opinion.

"By the way, it is advisable, even though you might possibly win the prize, to put off your trip indefinitely. There is a fatal and mysterious illness in the air called legionnaires' disease. As another famous author says, there's a 'figure in the carpet' that nobody can figure out. In fact, there's a 'beast in the jungle' too, so you can just imagine how we have to watch our step. I've even had to sell my Honda.

"Here is a more recent picture. Do you think it looks like me?" I seal the envelope. Excuse me, Reggie J.

Later in the morning, leaving Sister listening to the ads ("I'm not thrilled with my laxative") and the cats helping Margarita succor another Death Wish fern she has found in the basement, I walk pleasantly and well-suited in my new blouse and old jumper down the six flights of stairs to the lobby floor. The front door is open and the elevator is in the basement, motionless; there are no sounds of repair work. But the postman has been and the day's mail is waiting (again?). Purina, forestalling, is definitely not interested in any more cat pictures on stepladders or anywhere else; they have their own photographers, also their own dieticians. Channel Thirteen needs money again, though, and Pen Pal has written a surprise letter: he *has* won the contest and will call me when he arrives in New York.

Seeking help, I raise my eyes to the Bulletin Board and read: "How is your Urim? Have you examined your Thummim lately? Take your troubles to Dr. H.J." Unacquainted with Dr. H.J., I take them to Broadway instead and on the corner run into Mr. Felkin from Amsterdam House. Stiff-legged, like Rupert, he is trying to look alert, with bangs, as he watches the young girls pass in their long tight jeans and their adorable little sweaters.

My proposition is an intolerable intrusion on his privacy.

8

"Mr. Felkin, will you come to Nel Thompson's funeral, please?"

It's not only young men who hate to answer old women. This rancid old man drives a hard bargain for the favor. "What's she paying per head?"

"Nothing in the strict sense. It's a very short service. Music, flowers, and eulogy omitted. It's a cremation."

"It's a cheap cheat. I like to view the body. How's she gonna get resurrected you damn Christians think so much of, if she's cremated? How's she gonna get all those ashes together?"

"She'll have to work that out when the bugle blows."

"In a recycled pickle jar? How about fingerprints and dental work for identification in case somebody murders her beyond recognition?"

I look down the street at the garbage trucks by the Hunan Garden restaurant. Fumes are rising. "God could gather together all the gases."

"He'd have a lot to gather with that old gasbag."

"We'll probably go somewhere afterward for refreshments. Tom's, Moon Palace, or that Amy's place, eastern. Or Falafel. I know someone who works there."

"Stand up at a counter chewing shredded grass for that old bat?"

"Well, how about a place where you sit outside if it's sooty enough? There's one that hasn't been cited for violations in a long time."

Prolonged silence. Time is passing, and on the way to

the Philharmonic I want to get a glove for George. Margarita, intent on the fern, failed to find one in the basement. "All right, to our place, then. Shrimp, popovers, and bourbon."

"What time?"

"She's not dead yet."

"When do you expect?"

"Well, she's not even sick. But she doesn't look very well."

"She never did look very well and I'm busy that day," he says. "And you can't bury nuts too soon to suit me." He means me too. A rhythmist of the old school, he executes a fart in three-fourths time, lets the music die down to pianissimo, then waltzes back to the corner where the young girls pass.

Rejected by Felkin, I easily enlist Kirby in the Registrar and cross the street to get the bus to Lincoln Center. At the nearby fruit stand Bart Raither has just weighed out two more pounds of sweet potatoes.

"My sister, the learned librarian from Aix, says you're a fake. That you do it with a built-in computer."

"Your sister's smart for a woman, all right, but she's wrong this time. I practice on a scale at home."

I look at his hands, which now and then he flexes, spreading them far out, then bringing the fingers back to cup the palms. He pulls the fingers, stretching them, then bends them backwards toward his wrist. Pianists do this, it is said, also Cambodian dancers and stranglers. He is left-handed, I now remember with interest, and though he will never succeed in throwing a decent sidewinder, he may be able to furnish George with a right-handed glove.

He doesn't even *own* gloves anymore, he says. The weight of the glove, no matter the material, would ruin his sensitivity to the feeling of the potato; the grain would obscure the real texture and thickness of the potato skin. To become used to the weight of the glove in relation to the weight of the proposed potato, plus the changing weight of the moisture in the atmosphere, in the heavy fumes surrounding the fruit bins and garbage heaps of Broadway, would be too difficult. It would be like meddling with a delicately balanced instrument, like a trapeze walker wearing heavy shoes on a tautly strung wire.

Good God. Why do old men get so senile and old women stay so smart? "What are you trying to prove? That by acting like a nut, you're not really one?"

"I'm not trying to, and don't have to, prove anything. I'm picking up two pounds of sweet potatoes because it's something I like to do and I'm not hurting anybody doing it. And if you're out bumming for free gloves I've given all mine to the Salvation Army."

We part, laughing, as we have before, and I decide to walk to the Salvation Army shop at Ninety-sixth Street. In front of Falafel I pass Mr. Gamal. He does not speak, but a block farther a familiar voice does. "Would you buy me a hot dog? It's fifty cents." I look into the red eyes, at the crisp, neatly combed red hair, at the distressed shoes, at the man wearing them. He is clean, almost dapper. Obviously he bathes somewhere. Where? None of your business, the eyes answer. Do you think you own me because you force your money on me? Give me the money or not. He stands by the hot dog cart looking at me. His buttonless coat is the same color as his hair, as if he had once dressed with care, matching here or there, or not, as it pleased him. His air is cocky but the shoes are tired; he can last only as long as the shoes. He does not stoop to begging, there is no "please" in the question, though it is pleasantly put. He watches to see if I give the two quarters to the vendor or to him. The burned-out eyes do not blink. I hand the money to him, get a sincere "Thank you," and am ashamed to wait and see if the purchase is completed or if he stops another passerby.

It is a bright and cheerful day, an invitation to boyish pranks, and down a side street Pard is at another stall, picking up overturned books. He waves back at me and I now walk through the triangular little park with a recumbent lady in stone bidding one rest. Many of the SROs have come to sit on the benches as they drink from their bottles and feel the sun through the cluster of ginkgo trees. Some are not even drinking.

The Upper West Side is booming, report the boom watchers. Just look at it boom. I'm looking, and maybe it is, but it's hard to detect in most of the streets I pass. Though this is not the most interesting stretch in our neighborhood, being one hundred percent commercial Broadway, walking is an enjoyment to me, and many of the apartment houses on the side streets are seedily attractive. I am torn between looking down at the sidewalk for a find and gazing up at the buildings for one, a habit instilled in me by my architect brother. Scrolls like tired snails inch across some of the façades. Dolphins, bells, and rams' heads are popular pediment decoration. Urns and medallions draped with cement laurel chains frame the doorways. Carved artisans, crouched uncomfortably in squares, are squushed under cornices: a mason mixing his mortar, tongue hanging out as though to taste, a painter daubing at the easel, the architect's name on a T square with date of completion. It is many of these ornaments that are now deemed loose and dangerous and are removed or covered with the protective iron bars.

Erected in the early 1900s, some buildings are classically handsome, with lovely cornice lines and rounded windows. In others, arches and gables and dormers are frequent. Turrets occur, almost drunkenly. None of the buildings have courtyards, with fountains or attendants, as do the more Beaux Artsy ones a few blocks farther south, but a few have set-back entrances with flower boxes and central awning, and on the roof of one of these, divided—it's two parts with separate roofs—boys are shouting and throwing a small ball. The light is red, and I watch them. One, running, throws the ball too hard and over the open space to the roof next door. The others dare him and he pretends to jump after it, then, chicken, takes the long way around the cistern.

Fruit stands proliferate along the way, crowding the sidewalk. Yes, there're a lot of sweet potatoes in the world. You would almost have to practice weighing them at home —if you'd lost your marbles and were interested in that sort of thing. In front of one store an old man is playing "Doodle Doo Doo" on a mandolin. It doesn't sound any better than it did nearly sixty years ago, played right, and the man smiles a little at my offering. Down one side street a block fair is in slow progress. I stop a moment, ever intrigued by the things people decide they no longer want but someone else may—old family portraits (deframed orphans of the sidewalk), odd bits of cracked crockery, *Applied Analytics*, Erica Jong—never the right glove. At Ninety-sixth Street the large controversial lot where the Riviera Theater once stood, and Irene Bordoni sang "Let's Do It" uptown, has been planted in bright patches of zinnias, marigolds, and chrysanthemums and proudly dubbed Community Garden. Bloom. But it is already the announced site of a high-rise apartment complex. Boom.

By the defunct public comfort station in the middle of the street the derelicts and drunks are playing at tables they've set up by the benches. Bending over, the players, as well as can be seen from a distance, are fitting pieces of some sort into a kind of pattern. One leans over, tries a piece, others shake their heads and push him away; it is their turn now to try their own luck. A correct placement evidently occurs as I watch; there are congratulatory pats on the back and the paper-bagged bottle is passed.

An idyllic scene? Forgotten men playing with jigsaw cutouts of life in the middle of Broadway, still trying to fit into the puzzle? Pigeon shit. A man walks straight up the Ninety-sixth Street hill as if he intends to bump me. I embrace my purse and jump aside. He makes a sham grab and shows his teeth, not bad, though his uppers need attention, like mine. The clock across the street says the temperature is sixty-eight degrees Fahrenheit, twenty Celsius, and the hour one-thirty, hurrying time.

And now, enjoying the most beneficial of all the condescending crumbs thrown the elderly, I ride on my half-fare card to the Philharmonic. Two hours of Respighi, Moussorgsky, Elliott Carter, during whose nonmusical (to me) moments I work on Nel Thompson's list, compose a letter to Citibank regarding forged check, and try to think of all the Shakespeare sonnets beginning with "When" and "O" (ten Whens, twelve O's, for what it's worth). I also pick up some good stories to tell Sister at the Happy Hour: how all the freshly coifed ladies in our row still ask about her, how in the Moussorgsky Miss Hessel got mixed up on the pictures at the exhibition, thought the Polish Ox Cart was the Great Gate of Kiev, clapped too early, and got shished by Mrs. Myerson. How in the Elliott Carter the old ladies marched up the aisles with their coats. How the conductor waved his baton and the orchestra played louder. How the old ladies marched on. Do they have to catch a train? Are they bored stiff? Are they making a choice? Or do they all have to go to the bathroom—at the same time?

Will try to make this a philosophical debate and take

her mind off her weak drink. Stretch it out, try to make her laugh but not feel bad that she can no longer go. Remember to tell about the special old lady who tripped in the aisle in her hurry to get out. An usher rushed up to help her. She thought he was trying to stop her, wrestled him off, and went on, triumphant. To her judo lesson?

Or shall I tell her of the bus ride home? Of the woman who had let the drunk stranger sitting next to her sleep with his head on her shoulder, even going past her destination so as not to disturb him? Of how people smiled, watching? Or of the woman who, having misplaced her half-fare card, held up a similarly shaped card and was stopped by the driver, who made her pay full fare. "You are not using a good card," I told her when she sat down. "You should use this color," and showed her mine: my mother's Temperance card which, yellowed with age and held at the correct angle (thumb covering 1936, Rock of Ages imbedded in palm of hand), has gone as yet unchallenged.

"She hesitated too long," said someone across the aisle. "She should have pushed aside that little man in front of her."

"That little man had a two-blade knife in his hand," she said.

"We give you these nice cards and you don't respect them." Furious, the driver slammed into gear.

"We worked for what we get," she said. "And we shouldn't have to hold up anything."

Or shall I tell her of the little golden-haired angel, no older than eight, who called the driver "fucking bastard" when he would not hold the bus for her schoolmates? Or of the old man on a front seat who, without warning, screamed, loud and wrenching, then rested his chin on his cane and rode the rest of the way quietly?

Or shall I save a couple of items for George?

At home I forget to tell any of them. The lobby door is still open and a crowd of neighbors has gathered in the hall. Mrs. Harkness is dead and the door to her apartment sealed.

9

No foul play involved, unless you count natural causes. Not a mugging this time, either, just that old realized dread of dying alone, except that Mrs. Harkness had Ronny. Mrs. Ordway is walking him now, trying to find a home for him. She doesn't think her big cat would tolerate his competition, but she has tried to comfort him and has combed his hair. He is too dazed to care. When Mrs. Harkness had fallen, unconscious, it is assumed, she had apparently caught him, heavy, across his back. Not wishing to disturb her, or perhaps so pinned down he couldn't, he had not moved, and now with a high sobbing moan stumbles as he walks. Mr. Ordway walks him to Kirby, who starts phoning. Can Kate and I take in a third party? A loud "No" from Sister, who offers to pay his board elsewhere. This is not needed. Love is needed, and Mrs. Harkness's daughter, located, comes to take him.

At the Happy Hour, sad about Mrs. Harkness and Ronny and potentially in the same boat, Sister and I, to cheer up, decide to make Worcestershire sauce. On file in some "safe place" and lost to me forever, though it's also listed in my missing notebook, which I fear Margarita has donated to the basement, is a clipping from the New York *Times* that purports to be the Saga of a Sauce. An anonymous nobleman, it intimates, having served abroad, brought home the formula to the shire of Worcester. Well, Sister and I, who weren't born yesterday, or even the day before, recognize this as just another media lie to keep old ladies down. Our maternal grandfather, with whom we lived as children, invented it to put on his mutton and his little field peas and was not ashamed to give *his* name: Papa Scot.

"I remember the day he did it," says Sister. Me, too. I remember he did pour it out of a bottle before he invented it, though. But Sister has the clincher. "I remember the Tamarind Tree."

In those early Worcestershire-inventing days, 1914–16, we were the only people in our town with a tamarind tree. Many had pomegranates and figs bordering the boardwalk to the privy, with persimmons and chinaberries up front near the porte cochere (a name new to us, but catching on), and several had successfully transplanted chinquapin trees. But only we had the tropical tamarind, hard to grow, but not impossible in our East Texas climate. So romantic itself, so lilting, so like a song—Come tamar with me under the tamarind tree—it had come to us by default, and through an impulsively down-to-earth *un*romantic act of my grandmother, a high-minded local Latin scholar who thought my grandfather had married above him.

During the Civil War (we never called it War Between the States) and immediately afterward, my grandfather had been very young, hungry, thirsty, ignorant, and poor. On borrowed money he had opened a little general store, established credit with Mr. Percy, his wholesale Galveston connection, and with hard work, close dealing, and some luck in land and timber, prospered. Now old and able, still lacking in a few conjugations, English as well as Latin, he intended to eat and drink as he wished and did not mean to be stopped by anybody or anything, even impulsive acts of my teetotaling grandmother.

The argument advanced by interests of the liquor industry that teetotalers drive people to drink is not true in my grandfather's case. It is on record (Cole, his faithful henchman and our talented man-of-all-work) that his devotion to whiskey had begun long before he met my grandmother. Though noticed, this devotion did not interfere with his relations with the rest of the family (except with my grandmother) and he tried, without disturbing his own routine (toddy, nap, toddy, dominoes), to make little half-orphans feel at home. He nightly entertained us with stories of vicious panther attacks he had warded off with valor and sometimes bare hands. On birthdays he gave us Percy Presents from Galveston: fur-lined gloves for July, a miniature Haviland tea set when we had wanted an air gun, a silver barrette with a bad clasp when we had wanted snowshoes so we could get mal de raquette like the Camp Fire Girls. At Christmas he and I exchanged firecrackers: I handed him the five-cent package, he thanked me and punctiliously handed it back. We were even; both thought it was funny. And it was he who proudly distributed the award-winning silver dollars for spelling and declaiming and skipping grades, and to my sister Sue for athletic prowess.

But it was my grandmother, staunch defender of women, right or wrong, and my backer always, on whom I depended most. Rushing through her tonic to free the bottles for me to exchange for a new book at the drugstore, so tactfully tender with a child whose dog or cat had just been killed (she knew when to stop kissing or when not even to start), it was she, shameless encourager of a child scribbler, that, next to my mother, I loved the most and whose ablative absolute I admired above all others, even Sister's. In return she called me "Punkin" a lot, and seemed to mean it.

But there was a less predictable, less admirable side to her, too. She was convinced that a school-teaching knowledge of Latin and the chronicled deeds of her Mexican-fighting father entitled her to a more suitable mate than my grandfather, who had spent most of *his* Army life foraging for (stealing) food and drink, and whose ablative was absolutely nonexistent. Periodically she struck out at the marriage in which, it was no secret, her primary interest had been to help her chronicled, perhaps, but needy parents.

One day, throwing down the *Gallic Wars* and taking up one closer home, she emptied into the pig trough not only my grandfather's new case of Tennessee mash, but also that of his Lea & Perrins Worcestershire sauce. Instead of swallowing whole a freshly cut plug of chewing tobacco, as he had done when she had opened wide the big iron side gate and invited cows into his little field pea patch, he put down his toddy glass and watched, half-admiring, from the porch. Her aim was perfect, her hand steady. She did not spill a drop of either fluid. As a child of four I witnessed this scene but cannot vouch for its other particulars. I do know, though, that after he had quieted some excited old hogs, Grandfather rescued for his own use a bucket of the mixture and decided, in case the emergency (my grandmother) rose again, to thereafter make the sauce himself. Cole, good with concoctions on the back of the stove, could always provide him with a passable mash but not with an acceptable sauce.

His first step was to get in touch with Mr. Percy. Though it served chiefly now as a refuge for him and his domino-playing cronies, the little store was still his means of contact with the wholesale world. It was in his order to Mr. Percy for enough Lea & Perrins to see him through till his own first making that he included a request for tamarind, essential to the making of the sauce. (The label on the bottle said so.) Short on the spice pods my grandfather expected, Mr. Percy, never one to miss a sale, sent the next best thing, a whole tamarind tree another customer had returned. Six feet tall when it came, its roots bagged like athletes' privates, the tamarind was planted in the backyard near the well house where my grandfather stored, under lock and key now, the L&P, his tobacco, and his current supply of bourbon. Involved in an investment more face-saving than financial, he could sit here on a bench in the shade and, between naps and nips, watch his tree grow.

At first it languished and seemed to miss the gambling high life of Galveston port. Then the roots, reaching, recognized congenial soil and caught on. Handsome leaves spun out, and though not of the broad-based utilitarian variety vied for on Riverside Drive, were pinnates of a high order. The limbs strengthened, tempting the younger, more daring among us to chin them—forbidden by my grandfather. Do not touch the tamarind tree! The tree proved hardy, however, surviving not only our physical assaults but those of pronunciation—"tamar" as in "hammer," "rind" as in "bacon." ("Tamar" as a verb has come down in our usage to mean "to court," somewhere between "to smooch" and "to get down to real business.")

Grace, our tuneful washerwoman, called it the Tambourine Tree, but to most of us it was just another Percy swindle. Sometimes while our grandfather napped, we children, bribed by our elders, would dress up in the *too* old-fashioned corsets, the *too* outdated high shoes (frequently both for the same foot), the *too* outlandish feather boas that even the sharp-dressing ladies of Galveston had turned down and, while Grace beat a tin-pan tambourine, would flap our wings and chicken-waltz around the Tambourine Tree. Surprising us, our grandfather would swing his gold-headed cane in the air the way he did when possums got in the hen house, and call us all, including my mother and grandmother, "scalawags"—but enjoying it as much as we did. That was as mean as he ever got.

None of this irreverence seemed to affect the tree. It

flowered in spectacular orange and purplish bell-shaped blossoms, the envy of less exotic tree growers, and of which even my grandmother approved.

But it was the pods, citric, acid, laxative, and called Indian date by those who know their Arabic, or can read the encyclopedia, that gave my grandfather pleasure. Two years after the tree came to us, years in which we went through numerous cases of the name brand (we put it on *everything*), years in which I became six, Sue eight, my brother ten, and Sister twelve, he harvested the pods for his first sauce.

Thinking back to the rural simplicity of that first Worcestershire making, which I remember with only a few minor lapses, I am reminded in reverse of the Japanese Tea Ceremony (the Cathedral has a course in it) and its fussiness about the guests, the etiquette, the aesthetics, the teahouse, the exquisite pot with its traditional message in the bottom. My grandfather's pot was a big black iron one, with stubby, ugly feet. At different times it was used to boil the clothes, make the lye hominy, and scald the entrail casings for pork sausage. In between these duties, it stored water to nurture the little field pea patch through the dry spells. It was a busy pot, part of our everyday lives, and there was never time to read or even write any ceremonial messages in the bottom.

My grandfather's guests were captive, family who had been living off of him for years. Unlike their Japanese counterparts, they did not have to crawl in humility through a three-foot-square opening to get to the teahouse and would not have found a teahouse if they had, nor did they step nuance by nuance from this *ma* space to that *ma* space and squat, waiting only heavens knows how long, for, of all things, tea, not even iced. But they did crowd more or less irritated and half-humble in summer heat under the tamarind tree. My grandfather enjoyed the shade of the well house.

With a potential height of from sixty to ninety feet, the tamarind was now as tall as the chinaberries, with a short but strong trunk, and though for this occasion we were allowed to stand under it, we were still not allowed to touch it. It made a canopy over our heads, and a good thing, for I have read that on murky Hindustan nights the native species exudes a lot. A bit of a blusterer and show-off, my grandfather asked for full attendance, at least for this first making, and somewhat to his surprise got it. Widowed daughters, orphaned grandchildren, hanging-on kin, our three colored helpers and friends, Cole, Grace, and cook Bliss, cats, dogs, chickens, any neighbors who expected free sausage next fall, even my grandmother, cause of it all, felt obliged to appear.

Sister was hauled out, protesting, from her cool retreat under the high back steps where she had set up her library. This was after Whitman, and her new love was Horace—in the original, natch. While she read the Odes and the Epodes, with *Elsie Dinsmore* on the side, she ate cans of Vienna sausage and Del Monte pineapple, sharing the shade and the vittles with the more literate of the Rhode Island camerados, who had translated her *Drink at Your Peril* signs and knew she was a good person to hang around with.

Above us in the tamarind, a mockingbird reported on the proceedings—prink. All around us flies bit, dogs barked, hens cackled, and children giggled. Sultry vapors rose under the canopy of leaves. Trying to escape them, we stepped backwards into the chicken water receptacles, detached doors of old iron stoves. Looking like bad negatives of pictures seen in pictures, or dreams in which you participate but do not appear, we swatted out with our palmetto fans, and watched.

On the water shelf, a raised slab of marble on which in summer we ate watermelon twice a day, someone (Grace) had helped my grandfather line up the ingredients. From the bench where after refreshment he often sat to reassemble himself before facing my grandmother, my grandfather chunked them into the pot. First, anchovies. Mr. Percy regularly unloaded on my grandfather not only his leftover trees, sidesaddles, and iron gates, but more esoteric delicacies for which my grandfather, something of a sport (but more of a chump, said my grandmother), always paid and which his domino cronies devoured. Sometimes the old men's rejects trickled down to us children. Caviar (which the old men thought was roach turds and we thought was BB shot), spread on cold corn bread and dipped in buttermilk, was a one-time treat. After the anchovies came strained persimmons, some already setting for beer, then dried onions and shallots, salt, vinegar, sugarcane syrup, and ground dried field peas from his special patch by the plum orchard. When he added the pulverized tamarind pods there was a graceful though self-effacing kind of la-di-da of the fingers with which he lifted the pot lid (true, Grace had to help him lift it), sort of like a poet reading from his own stanzas, not really expecting them to work, but not starting off too bad. For, as they say in Japan, "Of the infinite number of ways in which the lid may be removed, only the most beautiful is insisted on." Nothing my grandfather knew, of course, nor did I till I read it so described by Jiro Harada in the Britannica. I think it was not an instinctive ceremonial grace that gave the moment a certain quack charm, but the tamarind acid stinging his tobacco-stained hands.

Last, or almost, he poured in a milk bucket full of bourbon. Dipping in with the long wooden spoon normally used to test the hominy, he stirred the mash till it was smooth and flowing freely. We all watched as he scooped up some of the mixture, blew on it, and while Grace, who was waiting for the pot for her clothes, accommodatingly held the spoon handle for him, took a loud, speculative sip. (Talk, unknown to me at the time, was that the long wooden spoon was not all that Grace ever held for him, that ingredients were not all she lined up, that pot lids were not all she helped lift.) After my grandfather, we all tasted. Difficult. The Japanese do it easier, sipping from the same bowl, the Tea Master passing the prettiest side of the bowl to face the guest, who does not drink from it so, but gives it a two-quarters turn. (Impolite, when you consider the trouble the Tea Master took to get it facing that way.) But we did it, each helping the other, backing off the full length of the handle and holding it steady and at mouth's height for the one after him to lap at the tasting end.

Cole, Grace, and Bliss, hoping this time for the usual discrimination, stepped aside, but my grandfather insisted they sip with us from the same spoon. We all partook, backing off, tripping on the stove doors, and bobbing awkwardly, like clumsy dancers in some slow, country pavane. Some meekly swallowed (this I saw), some retained the mixture, like a hospital pill, on the back of their tongue or parlayed it to some secret cavity (this I only assume). Holding the spoon where the contents were lowest and least likely to come in contact with her lips, my mother bravely swallowed. My grandmother kept her lips clenched. But no one, not even these two strong women, had the courage to ask this spoon to pass. All accepted it.

All except one. Already better read than most present, anxious to get back to her library under the house, her sash and the bow on her yellow hair wilting in the heat, Sister, when the spoon, my mother holding the other end, got to her, tasted the contents, gave the spoon the regulation two-quarters spin away from her, and knocked it across the yard into the chicken water. Looking my grandfather straight in the eye, she spat the spew at his feet.

"This is ridiculous," she lisped and, barefooted, kicked the sacred tamarind tree.

The kick did not hurt the tree, hardwood, but one of Sister's toes, still crooked, is called her Tamarind. But she gave no sign of pain as we watched her stomp off and disappear under the back steps, where later that day my grandfather hunted her out and gave her a silver dollar. The sauce-making had become a bore even to him. He was getting thirsty and sleepy and Grace wanted the pot so she could get on with her clothes. But he had one more ingredient to add, one that gave the sauce not only coloring and preservative, but his opinion of the whole affair.

Is it that lack of tobacco juice that makes the bought imitation stuff so tame and tasteless, that leaves the New York *Times* clipping so dull a saga? Is it the pot, or is it the memory of that spicy, gamy odor of tamarind, persimmon, and hog guts that clothes boiled in it gave off for months afterward? Is it because, like Bart Raither picking up sweet potatoes, my grandfather was simply doing something peculiar he wanted to do and was not hurting anybody else by doing it? Or is it because he made the sauce only when half-drunk and, though it never occurred to us then, because he was possibly as sad and lonely as we—the reason he also made up the panther stories? (One had come out of the woods, eyes flashing, teeth gnashing, and talked Panther Latin at him. Another had slept with him, shoving him from the bed and snoring so loud he'd had to get up and take a toddy. Another had brought all her kinfolks, three dozen, with her, and they had eaten not only all the food in sight but the tables and the chairs, too, though spitting out the screws.)

More than any of these, I think what makes his homemade Worcestershire special is Sister standing there, foe of the phony, seeing it plain and daring to tell it like it was.

It all went back to Whitman and Miss Roxie. Seeing the flagpole topple that day, catching her between the piledriver and the derrick, two of her more intricate occupational gestures, she had seen the truth. Way up there, alone, at the top of the derrick, she had had time to think. For she not only had to bring her right fist up and down in quick succession driving in the piles, some of them quite obstinate and not that well cut, she then had to reach up on tiptoes, spreading the fingers of each hand to meet at the top of the derrick, a gesture that helped her later in basketball but tore out a lot of her middy blouse sleeves. Up there, Old Glory crumpled at her feet like a worn bandanna, she had been liberated. Watching the plane plop down on the croquet grounds, seeing the wickets and the sunbonnets fly, she had heard the talk of Miss Roxie's turning eye-balls and it had set her free.

An addlepated old woman now, leaning on her walker, favoring her toe, Sister says that somehow our making of the sauce raises her spirits and seems important to her.

For, of course, as in the Tea Ceremony, it is not the sauce itself that is important but the making of it, the old journey-not-the-destination saw. Kept in a demijohn in the well house and left to "work" for six months, my grandfather's sauce was unsavory, inadvisable, downright stinking, and eventual chicken feed. Sister's and mine is not that much better, not nearly as good as Lea & Perrins and never meant to be. Instead of tobacco juice we use strong tea. Tamarind is available in oriental shops and in liquid form at bodegas, but we settle for stale white wine. For sweetening we empty our shelves of accumulated honey—why do gift bearers think all old ladies like white wine and honey? Last we add a splash of Lea & Perrins itself. For a pot we use the wok, bent but serviceable, which Margarita found in the basement and in which, when not sauce-making, we store the duplicate keys we keep for friends and neighbors. Stir-frying, it takes us twenty minutes from wok to bottle. It took my grandfather two hours.

We seal the sauce in empty caper bottles, small, but the sauce is strong and we have noticed that people are apt to refuse outright a larger portion. Sister, trying to spoon the sauce into the tiny opening with her trembling hands, becomes impatient, says it's ridiculous, gives her walker an exasperated kick, and hurts her Tamarind Toe. Monica, our neighbor, who had come to borrow one of Margarita's little pieces of wood to put in her window where the air conditioner doesn't fit, but who had stayed to help us bottle, brings her a Toe Tie, a kind of adjustable elastic support left over from a sales job she had had during the Depression when she had the exclusive Toe Tie concession for the whole Southeast Seaboard. Sister says it's ridiculous, claims it's too big for her fine patrician toes, and throws the tie to the cats, who, searching for catnip, demolish it.

Monica is not offended and says she has more; part of her pay was in Toe Ties. She uses them for quite a few things, wears her folding money in one, tied not to her toe but to her bra strap, with a tiny but efficient mousetrap attached. She has learned to walk evenly, regally, and to avoid potholes so the trap, unbaited but set, will not snap. Many compliment her on her queenly posture and I have seen models on TV who could take a lesson from her bearing. If anybody except her reaches up there they sure get a surprise. Somebody who robbed her in the elevator is now running around with the tip of his finger missing, like the man in *The Thirty-nine Steps*. Even leaning over, bottling, she has excellent posture. But in her hurry to be the good neighbor she has not firmly enough closed the door at which Mr. Huang now appears, lugging Martha. "She's chewing our hanging fern and digging up our bean sprouts." Before we can press a gift upon him, he throws Martha inside and retreats.

Back at the wok, Monica, claiming a bad pancreas she got on a job selling cosmetics in Baltimore (she now uses only Vaseline and corn oil on her skin), also refuses the gift bottle and takes her fine posture home. Carrying the rejected bottles to store away for surprise stocking stuffers, I meet an old friend. He has the dazed, proud look of the much traveled (Boy, have I been around!) and would dally in the hall, but the cats behind me pounce and he makes the quick right turn.

I hear the splash, slam down the lid, and in holding back the cats spill a dab of leftover sauce on the floor. Ten minutes later when I go to clean it up, the cats have forgotten the mouse and are gazing at the sauce. Roaches, dead as raisins, infest it. Sister and I have made a great breakthrough in extermination. While I watch, amassing a fortune, the roaches, like the old ladies at the Philharmonic, rise as though on signal and dash off.

I wash the wok and, hidden under the ceremonial cat hairs and overlooked keys, get the bottom message: Pen Pal.

10

"Hank?"

The cats have never heard Nigerian English before (nor have I) and crowd close to the phone. "Hank's out of town. How are you, Geoffrey?"

"Is this Auntie?"

Apparently convulsed at the "Auntie" touch, embellished with the broad, broad A, the cats roll off the bed. "Yes, this is Auntie." I wink at my friends as I give him back his broad A. "It's so good to hear from you. Hank is not here. Is this a long-distance call from Nigeria saying you can't come? I'm so sorry."

"No, Auntie. Perhaps Hank has not told you. I've won the prize and am here to read my essay."

"That's lovely, dear. And what is the title of your little piece?" I steady myself on the edge of the bed and wait for it.

"How High Can It Go Before It Has to Come Down? Is World Power Built on It Exclusively? Why Waste It? Can Man with All His Technical Expertise Devise a Satisfactory Substitute?"

The cats look at me: This is a *title?* "You mean that's the whole essay?"

"No, Auntie. Other concerns are: Should Young Men Go to War for It? How About Young Women, Are They Not Equally Concerned? Is Offshore Exploration Feasible? How Do the Middle East and African Nations Compare in Capacity and Natural Resources?"

The prize, he says, includes hotel accommodations and

entertainment for which he and his tutor, Mr. Akabu, had hoped Hank would join them. They have a lot to discuss. "When will Hank be here?"

"How long will *you* be here, dear?"

"A week, Auntie."

"Oh, Hank unfortunately will be away much longer. Spring training."

"Isn't October rather early for spring training, Auntie?"

"Not for Hank, dear. He's very special, being so young. His fast ball is so fast they had to give him a handicap. He has to practice with a five-pound weight on his wrist."

There's a sizzling at the other end of the wire. Or is it muffled Nigerian giggles? I hold on and hear Geoffrey say, "But Hank and I have so much to talk about. Notes to compare. And other things. I especially wanted to introduce him to a new friend I've made in this country. Did he get my letter?"

"I don't know, dear. He has so much correspondence with different ball teams and advertisers. So many want him to endorse their products."

"Was his decision to go to spring training sudden, Auntie?"

"Oh yes, dear, very." Almost simultaneous with your call. "He'll be sorry to miss your essay. But may I come instead?"

"Oh, Auntie, of course. I'm very anxious to meet you. Though I feel like I know you already from Hank's description of you."

"Really?" What is this put-on-accent African talking about?

"I hope you enjoy the essay, Auntie. We have slides to illustrate my strongest points."

I bet. "I wouldn't miss it."

But after dinner Sister stumbles, almost falls, and I decide not to go. Indeed you will, she says; these stuck-up cats are all the company she needs. Ssz ssz. I finally agree to go and alert Monica to be on call.

This is an occasion, like most others, for which I do not have the proper clothes, so I shake the cat hairs off the blouse, tie on a skirt that Martha, constant kneader, uses to "make up biscuit," and start for the low life. With only the address, not the name of the hall, I taka the tax, as Margarita would say. The driver, a low-looking lecher whose eyes seem to be hanging out over his glasses, though he is not wearing glasses, looks at me surprised when he hears it. As if I were not the type, as if my Something were not all that Suitable, as if my Urim were not right up there with my Thummim, as if my Channel Thirteen tote with the gifts of H. James, W. Whitman, and honey were not the acceptable selections here. I appear nonchalant (to myself) during the journey, with no apparent concern for the soaring meter, and, arriving at the address, overtip grossly.

A doorman escorts me to the elevator, a liveried attendant accompanies me to the fifty-third floor and to a very elegant hall in a very high-rise building in a very rich neighborhood. How long has this been going on, I wonder? Where are the cops? What of the law? ERA and Abortion have trouble getting passed, and look at this. Is it known to what extent these thugs have taken over the city, how big a business this has become? To what extent is it underground? Do they pay taxes? No wonder the city's in debt.

A smiling usher shows me to a seat near the platform. In spite of their trade, the people present are not that bad-looking, I have to admit. They are totally without that sleazy exterior of their Times Square counterparts. All are in evening dress, no pickups off the $4.99 racks here. Certainly the three young men on the platform are very earnest-looking fellows as they sit behind their banners: 1st, 2nd, 3rd. Though not exactly 4-H or Christian Endeavor material, they look to be very healthy, outgoing types. When they do their tricks, will they use the banners, I wonder again, like raincoats?

This is my maiden visit to a high-class porn club or even to a low-class one, and I sit back, ready to be titillated. The program is in progress, and if they do it like "Miss America" the two runners-up have taken their bows first.

Numero Uno rises. He is shy yet poised, confident but modest, medium size and weight, very black, very young, and his old broad-A Auntie watches him with the fierce pride of adopted kin.

He is a slow starter but his act is superb. He knows the importance of anticipation. In that accent that wowed the cats he gives us a background history of his country and his people. He examines tribalism and ethnicity. He calls names—Yoruba, Hausa, Ibo, he reels off the many languages and dialects. He cites the colonial influences, British, French, German, their interest in the slave trade, the palm oil trade. We hear of treaties, and advance to the present-day government. We get a rundown on Education—not bad for those who are able to get it. We get the position of Women—improving, but still not good for many except as traders in the market. We get a strong hint why: polygamy.

We turn to religion. Many tribes have their local religions though adopting Christianity and Mohammedanism. They do not "eat religion," as in the old Chinese phrase, but adapt it to their own needs. The strict universal Moslem ban on alcohol has been modified in Nigeria to mean only ginger beer, associated with pagan rites. I reflect a moment on the meaning of this: Mr. Gamal is the only Moslem of my acquaintance. Geoffrey is a born-again Methodist.

Finally our essayist motions toward the slide machine, run by an older young man who must be Mr. Akabu, his tutor, the lights dim, and the illustrations begin.

I wait. This kid is a teaser.

First he gives us a glimpse of the countryside. We see palm trees and rubber trees in the rain forests, we see acres of small groundnut farms. We visit the busy cities, Lagos, Ibadan. We see the people laughing, dancing the high life, working, crying. We see them at sport—the great runners, the soccer players. We visit the open-air stalls of the Market Mammies, we see the food, the beautiful colored cloth, the local crafts, and calabash baskets everywhere. We see the museums and ancient regal sculpture. We see the colonial architecture of the government houses. We see the mosques and the Moslems at prayer.

I wait. If it weren't all so interesting it could get real boring.

We see civil war, starving children, and grieving parents. We get figures and charts and graphs. We get the full count on the GNP and the GAO. Then we're off on the highway again. We see the many cars and the traffic jams. We see the hope of the country—the big tankers low in the water. Then we go to the great oil fields of northern Nigeria, and light dawns: this joker is into Petrol, not Porn. Oil is bigger than Sex, and loaded with statistics.

As he carries his prize-winning thoughts past the long titles, Geoffrey takes the revered word *Petrol* and, like the greeting card makers who milk dry that other sacred six-letter word *Mother*, assigns attributes to each letter in it:

P—Potentials, Price, Possible Substitutions, Peanut Oil, Performance

E—Ethyl, Expertise, Energy, Environment

T—Techniques, Technology

R—Regulation, Rationing, Resources

O—Occidental, Opportunity, Offshore, OPEC, Options

L—his summation. He makes a big pitch on "LĒAD *not* LĔAD" and I am relieved to see he is as big a cornball as Hank.

The lights go up again. People rise and clap. As he stands by his large winner's banner Geoffrey bows toward the defeated contenders, the audience, then toward me, sharing his triumph with old Auntie. We are at the formal reception of the multinational petroleum consortium, sponsors of the essay contest. What I had thought was a statue in indecent pose is a gleaming stylistic gusher; what I had mistaken for a map of the porn district is a directory of the contributing countries.

"Auntie." Geoffrey smiles and we go to each other as though it were written down somewhere. (What *had* that Hank written?) We shake hands vigorously. "I did not know this was a subject in which you were interested, Auntie. I hope it was not tiring." Mr. Akabu is with him. The two smile at each other. This Akabu is a cool cucumber. I have a strange feeling that behind their irreproachable manners they are having a good me-young-black you-old-whitey laugh on old hayseed Auntie.

"Your nephew Hank has written of your great age and infirmities, but also of your keen interest still in world affairs and people. In what makes things tick."

This kid is laying it on too thick. Mr. Akabu's parting words confirm a quote growing suspicion unquote. "Yes, we enjoy Hank's letters so much. Tell him to work on his writing, though, on his style and content. His many allusions to other writers' sayings is cheap substitute for original thought."

The crowd is growing impatient to meet Geoffrey now and pushes politely forward. "Won't you stay for the reception, Auntie?"

"No, no, thank you so much. I must go now. My sister is not well."

He looks at me, surprised. "There is another auntie, Auntie?" Two aunties in the same sentence. Watch his own writing. "Yes, there is." You little jerk. There is the old queer.

"Thank you for coming, Auntie. Thank you for everything."

For a moment we look each other straight in the eyes, a beautiful black orb and a bloodshot old bifocal. There is a close, silent moment: I ask his pardon, he thanks me for trying. Then we exchange gifts and resume our former roles. "Please take these presents for yourself and Hank and tell him that perhaps my new friend and I can call on him in spring training camp. My friend is also a ballplayer, though older than Hank."

He delivers the old-lady kiss and the crowd claims him. I watch him as, gracious and at ease, bestowing, taking, smiling, serious, he accepts plaudits and parries questions. This petrol pusher is a comer. In two or three years when he is President/King/Chief of All Africa, parts of the USSR, and Outer Mongolia, I hope I am not too dead to be his Resident Auntie Liar.

The doorman calls me a cab and I take the new soccer ball and underground high life record home to Sister in my beautiful new calabash basket. The front door is open, the elevator is not running. The lobby is empty. I wait a moment on the bench, hoping a tenant will come in and accompany me up the stairs. *Do We All Have to Be Murdered Before This Thing Is Fixed?* asks the Bulletin Board and I start up the stairs. It is nearly eleven and most people have put out their garbage. On each landing I stop to pant, listen, look cautiously ahead and behind, before going on up the stairs, dirty, dangerous, dark. At the sixth floor I think I hear someone behind me and hurry on up the stairs, door key in fumbling hand with soccer ball and records. I wield the calabash like a weapon, anticipating Sister's What are you doing, swinging out with that crazy big gourd? Opening the door, I rush in and turn the locks. The cats meet me, crying. I push the desk in front of the door and follow them.

Sister is lying unconscious on the floor of her room.

11

Days of wild screaming follow. "I want to get out of here, I want to get out of here." Her vocal cords have not been affected by the stroke and, to compensate for the loss of mobility in her legs, seem rather stronger. Also her lisp is cured. "I don't know where I'm at, I don't know where I'm at." But her grammar is shot. "Leave off the 'at,' Sister," I say dumbly, "and look at this picture of Pen Pal and Reggie J. in the paper this morning. 'Essay winner gives a few pointers on Petrol to American League Big Car Owner.'" "I want to get out of here, I don't know where I'm at." "Sister, if you don't know where you're at, how do you know you want to get out?" "Because I don't know where I'm at. Help, help."

The kids on the street begin to mock her as they do the soprano. In the next house new tenants whose apartment adjoins ours bang on the thick communal wall. "Quit beating that poor old woman," someone shouts. "We'll get the police." Sister screams again, and Monica (who does not wear the bra trap at home) and I, as we had done the night of her stroke, half pulling and half carrying, get her out of their hearing into the next room. Sister fights all the way, strong hands up in front of me, feinting, guarding, a carry-over from playing running center in college basketball. We lift her into my mother's old hospital bed and with some difficulty put up the bars. She lies in a heap, motionless, panting. Her opponents on the basketball court had said that sometimes she had played so violently they had been afraid. But I know that all she ever wanted was to win.

Our sister Sue calls from Texas to say she feels well enough to come help, but without too much fight agrees to wait till her regular spring visit. For a while, with Dr. A.'s advice, I am able to take care of Sister alone.

It's only when she refuses to eat that I visit the nursing home. An old man comes to the sidewalk and throws part of his breakfast roll to a sparrow. "Hello, little fat pardner," he calls, "see you tomorrow." Another has drawn his wheelchair close to the fence where he can watch all who pass, and speak if they look his way. We talk for a moment, then at the lobby desk I sign in and pass through the large parlor room where the residents, like many of us everywhere, sit out their lives waiting for pills and meals. In front of the two elevators by the TV room I watch them come and go.

"Quit staring at *us*, and do something useful for *yourself*." A peppery old lady shoves a wheelchair at me and I help one or two residents off the elevator and into the pill place. On one elevator an old man tells me to hurry. He is punching all the buttons but never gets off, no floor suits him, nor anything else about the whole setup. Two others place bets on which elevator will come first. In the small bar a couple of regulars have gathered for the before-meal booster. "Your damn wheelchair is taking up all the room. I can't get my feet under the table," says one. "Put 'em on top, then," says the other, lifting her glass. Next to the ones who have their right minds but no place to go with them, it is the wispy, lost ones, the ones in the corners, that grab your heart. As I leave, an old woman in white socks and pink sweater suit follows me to the door. "Oh, no one wants me but you. Have you come to take me away?" "Not today," I say sadly and close the door. She is not allowed outside.

The Home, a haven for the helpless and hopeless, is not

so for many others there, and is definitely not for Sister. Nor even in extremis did I ever have any right so to consider it, and Dr. A. sends her instead to the hospital, where she spits out her pills at the nurses and becomes well known in her corridor. The various tests prove no new physical disabilities beyond the partial paralysis and the hampered heart. Her eyes are good, with extraordinarily strong muscles, and her back muscles the same, her reach, in spite of the paralysis, astonishing. After the spinal tap confirms the neurologist's previous diagnosis of advanced brain atrophy or Alzheimer's disease, all has been done that can be, and the nurses' aides are glad to see us go. One calls Sister a big mess; Sister is not too atrophied to fire back at her, "That makes two." Her roommates are kinder; one is comatose.

At home Dr. A. advises nurses around the clock. How will they get there, such a little clock, barely functional, a Whelan bargain, and one of the nurses quite large? I try to share this poor joke with Sister, but she is staring at the ceiling now, listening to someone there with a better one.

The nurses, on three eight-hour shifts, despise one another, meet briefly, and communicate in writing regarding pills and Pampers. Though distinct personalities, all women are graduates of some nurse's aide school, sport a semiliterate, paraprofessional lingo, say "flatus" instead of "gas," and have wigs galore. All are dependable and never complain of how many times, dressed, wig of the day in place, ready to go, they have had to stop, change the bed, and reassess the alignment of chucks and Pampers. They complain only of one another. All vie to see who can say "darling" the oftenest, are nice to the cats, but wish that we would fix up more and live classier so they could brag of it to their friends. All are proud of Sister's body, small, still firm, though becoming emaciated and dehydrated; her once too substantial legs with flying buttresses of Vienna sausage and Del Monte pineapple have whittled down to a shapely though still bowed calf. Her feet are narrow and, except for the Tamarind, with straight, youthful-looking toes. She takes five pills daily which must be mashed into soft food and given at different hours. Her throat is full of gunk that keeps making itself because of dehydration, but that each nurse says is the other two's fault.

All three become our friends.

By late October the fierceness is gone, but Sister's eyes, questioning, follow one accusingly about the room. We are relieved when they light instead on the pictures on the walls: Fra Angelico's "Annunciation," a Turner poster, a field of bluebonnets painted pretty well and mighty blue by a Dallas classmate. "The Musicians" (Giorgione?), which we both once professed to find so spiritual, gets more attention: why is that sappy-looking fellow at the keyboard looking over his shoulder at the string man as if he'd just felt a roach run up his back? Mostly she studies her own designs she has found on her flower-figured sheet—dogs of various breeds and poses, insects with spread wings, clouds to fly on. She shows some to Elizabeth and me, but most she keeps to herself, private. If she loses them in the pattern she searches anxiously till she finds them again, then looks quickly away as if to throw us off the scent. Gazing at the ceiling, she listens for another good joke. Nothing can top a good joke on the ceiling.

When she talks, hardly audible, it is of dying, though not calling it such yet. She is going on a long trip, says she doesn't want to go, but has to. It's not like any of her other travels, like to Aix or where she got the pictures. It's another place too far to come back from and she must get her things together to pack. She tells Cora, who has nursed her through other illnesses, that she wants her to go with her.

Cora thanks her for the invitation and, though honored to be the one chosen, politely declines, but will try to meet her later. Sister smiles a little at this. She no longer tolerates her dentures and says she will not take her toothbrush, or extra toilet paper, a former must for foreign travel, but will wear her Phi Beta Kappa key, which might come in handy if she loses her American Express card. Whether she believes in life after death, or that the spirit takes flight instead of making a dull thud, she has never really said. I know what I believe, but she is more religious, or less non-, and often used to sit in the huge nave of the Cathedral, alone except for the tourists taking pictures.

A few weeks pass with our lives centering around the nurses' shifts, the mail, phone calls, visits from neighbors, and news from friends. Slammed against the altar railing as she is contributing to the poor box, Kate Frazier is mugged on schedule. She is lucky this time; the Lord is with her; he does not let her fall. Mr. Gamal, Nel Thompson reports, has taken his samples and without warning moved from her building, leaving no forwarding address. All very suspicious, which reminds her, when is the New York *Times* printing my pigeon piece?

We have our regular phone calls: Ray (no, I do *not* remember the time the fashionable Claremont Inn refused us entrance because my dress was not something suitable), Torch (no, we do not need any more of those expensive light globes), and the daily nuisance who hangs up as soon as we answer. George calls to say another roommate has died, seven in all, and he receives a single room. Will I please send him one hundred aspirin, cement to hold his teeth in, fifty dimes for his phone calls, three Fruit of the Loom shorts, and six safety pins, medium size? Some of his zippers are going.

Martha's checkup shot is due and Monica helps me tote

her in our carrier to the vet, a few blocks away. An old couple is in the waiting room with their dog. Brown and sad-eyed, like them, he lies at their feet. A large lump shows on one leg. "It's cancer," says the woman, and looks at the man. They are desolate. "There's nothing to help," he says. "I wish it could be me instead." He leans down and hugs the dog. Waiting for the Judas needle, the dog licks his hand. Inside the examination room Martha gives Dr. F. a good clip when he gets too fresh. This is not the kind of visit she had in mind at all.

On social security day all the mailboxes of our tenants over sixty-five are broken into and robbed. Sister's and Mr. Loewenstein's checks go directly to the bank, mine is missing. But "Robert Penn Warren and the Vanderbilt Fugitive/Agrarians," a paper by Clark Banks, a young professor friend at the University of Tennessee, is intact, as are the usual Begs, Bills, and Rejections. Purina returns the snapshots (yes, they meant woks and sidesaddles, too). Con Edison, knowing full well elderly ladies rarely keep their kilowatts about them, gives us the same old run-around: if we still think the bill is too high, send all the back stubs with complete data. Channel Thirteen needs money. Pen Pal, back home, is working on a new essay, and Sherry, our schoolgirl in Mississippi, is selling those dollar-and-a-half-each shelled pecans again. Her class is raising money for a trip to China. Prices are up, stocks are down, Citibank remains positive that the check was not forged, and the monthly statements show an alarming decrease in our accounts.

The nurses have become an expensive proposition. We lack "unfortunately," as our friend H. James puts it, "a certain independence of the pecuniary sort," and even with generous insurance I grow fearful our modest savings will not last. As Sister sleeps most of the time now, Dr. A. says it's safe to "let" the night nurses go. Cora will continue coming from eight to five each day, and on call, and I now take care of Sister's few needs at night. She hates me for the things I am glad to do for her. Sometimes when she pretends sleep I feel her eyes following me about the room, resenting it all (Let me die and get out of here), yet sometimes she smiles.

Mostly she lies quietly, looking at the ceiling.

12

By November the trees on Riverside are stripped and beautiful. A provident (greedy?) squirrel carries three peanuts at a time, packing them as neatly as Altman parcels and burying them in, to me, poor places—behind a beer can, on top of another squirrel's stash. The jay lingers longer each day and I increase the food supply. The robin hops off as if not present; I pretend not to see him hiding in the brush and, fresh out of worms, leave him some cat food, Dixie Dinner, carried for that purpose. At home the mouse is in residence again behind the sack of birdseed.

It snows. "No heat on Thanksgiving?" says the Bulletin Board. "No hot water? Why? No one told them we were people."

In the Bronx, George has a dream of his childhood days on East 112th Street, where as lookout and pro rata man he had announced, at five cents a chip, horse droppings to the manure-needy gardeners of his street. He dreams of horses passing on the cobblestone street, clop, clop, clop, and of his responsibility to assign the prized droppings to the right person at the right time. "Another one for you, Mrs. Schleybein." "Your time, Mrs. Flusstein." Or the horses do not turn into his street at all, choosing that of a rival. "No, no, this street," he calls out anxiously in his sleep. "This street." And wakes up, an old man on a wet bed in a nursing home.

The little Jesus moon, the loveliest of the year, comes out. Christmas draws nearer. The desk by the door is heaped with packages to deliver, delighting the cats. Some packages we are even allowed to keep, but besides bed jackets and fancy food, who can think of something new to send old ladies? Very few; old ladies should be thankful to get anything, particularly all this nice white wine and honey. But there are a few specials: Cousin Charlotte sends divinity candy packed in egg cartons, with magnolia leaves and a camellia. Sue sends East Texas ribbon cane syrup in a half-gallon can. A pretty can, says Sister, who will taste the syrup on the hot-flavored country sausage Cousin Ross sends along with bottles of rose hips and vitamin C tablets to counteract the red pepper. He also sends another good chimney stuffer, *Nana*. Martha watches me squeeze it in by *The Red and the Black* and Books in Print. Clark Banks's article he read recently at the Modern Language Association meeting arrives: "Allen Tate and the Vanderbilt Fugitive/Agrarians." Sister looks down from the ceiling: That's a Christmas present?

We bottle-swap and send bought fruitcake or Texas Chewies to a few friends, then call it Merry Quits. Beth Gottchalck brings down a miniature herb garden, soon devoured by the cats, that she has grown for us in half-pint pots. The key and the package people come across handsomely with cookies and flowers, though there are the usual duds—handkerchiefs when we were counting on booze, a book about cats when we had hoped for a good mystery story. Bart Raither dumps another bag of sweet potatoes on us and I pass it on to Eddie Fuller with the Worcestershire sauce disguised in holly paper. Ella Maria Wodowski, a disabled neighbor, drags great bags of Christmas rolls and bread for me to take to the birds; her Polish friend at the deli is in charge of baked goods.

On Broadway I walk under the gloomy protective roofing and wait by the children's books stall. Boys pass, handle the books, jostle, and go on. Still no Pard. On

Christmas Day Ray calls, drunk, and wants to remember when we used to go to the Savoy Ballroom. The big bouncers would not let you stand still on the dance floor. "Keep moving, keep moving." Did they use prodders? I've forgot. He has a new kitten, Pooky Pie. Sue calls, celebrating: it's been four years since her mastectomy. She's almost made it. Margarita "cooka da turk" and brings us Christmas dinner, as does Cora—heartwarming, delicious with Ella Maria Wodowski's rolls and Eddie Fuller's sweet potato/Worcestershire pie. George, thanking for the candy and the *TV Guide*, sends us, out of his forty-dollars-a-month allowance, money for bourbon.

It is now just two months and two weeks since my last (latest) mugging. The notices have stopped coming, but I have three months and two weeks till I'm due. Rachel Rosen is mugged by a fellow student on the way home from her calligraphy lesson. It is the end of the term and neither goes back to class.

On New Year's Eve Eddie Fuller has a jam session at his apartment, and when Sister is asleep I go for a while. The joint is jumping; so is the filter in the fish tank. The fish swim back and forth, butting their noses against the glass, crazy with jive. A girl sits by me and says she feeds live mice to her iguana. Outraged, I move to another seat, then remind myself that I buy tender young spider plants for the cats' salad. Is it any different? You bet. The combo plays "Happy Birthday"—the big 0—and now I am really old.

The year is new but that's about all that is, though the Philharmonic does have a new rule: no latecomers admitted until the whole of the first number is finished. They can keep 'em out but they can't keep 'em in; the old ladies still march up the aisle. I find a dead bird, stiff in the snow. Taps for Cindy, too, I'm afraid; her lost-dog sign has rotted on the post and been replaced by that of Hal—"rather sad, brown, medium-sized with baggy ears, shaggy tail, and drooping left eyelid." (When, I wonder, will they start putting up the names of runaway children or missing old people?) The elevator is broken. The phone rings and rings: Estelle, our handicapped girl from Torch, to sell light globes (how can she always be so sure I'm in the tub?); Nel Thompson, to ask if my roach piece has come back yet; Ray, drunk, to remember what the speakeasy man wrote on my ID card—was it "Ragazza bionda, grande faccia lunga" or "grande faccia tunga"? George has a dream about Sister. She meets Mrs. Schleybein, and Mrs. Schleybein lets her try out her shovel. They seem to hit it right off, and it makes George feel good.

Someone steals the gas, rationed, expensive, and hard to find, out of Eddie Fuller's Chrysler.

Our good neighbors the Gottchalcks retire, move to Petaluma, California, and leave us their fans and pot plants.

We have our monthly meeting with most rewarding happenings (I name Pard) and local muggings noted. Mrs. Comer reports herself now eligible to join our club: waiting on the corner for the dog named Stanley, she is pushed inside a telephone booth, beaten with a baseball bat, and robbed. Stanley, watching from a safe distance, takes a double pee, makes sure she's out cold, and moseys on to another corner. In a SRO building across Broadway, resident thieves tie a pillowcase over a sick tenant's head, cut the telephone wire, steal her purse and TV, and leave her without water or food till the social worker comes. She is afraid to go to a home. We vote to try to help. How? A woman wrapped in a blanket has begun sleeping on the sidewalk of our street. She does not beg but accepts money for coffee. Found dormitory shelter, she calls Nel Thompson a dirty, meddling bum and picks out another street. We decide to leave her alone except for the coffee.

Mr. Gamal has surfaced and is on the street almost as much as the redheaded beggar and me. He has lost his job at Falafel but is too proud to beg ever, even without a "please"; his contempt for old ladies will see him through. The redhead, still trading on the Christmas spirit, has hiked his prices. "Could you give me sixty cents for a cup of coffee, and for seventy-five I could get a doughnut too. But if you don't have it, I can get it from somebody else." Now he is patronizing me. Lately I pretend not to see him and cross to the other side of the street. His hair, longer, is curly and covers his head like a cap. His shoes are mostly soles.

Pard has not been at the bookstalls in weeks.

Snow again. No heat. I pile the blankets on Sister. The cats lie on my chest and legs, using me as a warmer, or are they really trying to cut off my circulation? We stay in bed till the finches send out an emergency call: the sunflower seed on the sill is too soggy for them to flip open. Help! When I open the window to put out the dry seed a cardinal is waiting with the finches. I can*not* believe it, but shoo the cats out of the room and hurry to tell Sister. When I tiptoe back to the window he is gone. I scatter more seed in Sister's window, hoping he will come there. He doesn't, but the finches clinging to the railings loudly urge us on. Some of their little red heads have white caps of snow. Their chatter grows louder and Sister, her bird-watching span short, tells them to hush; she is listening to someone important on the ceiling.

Across the street two supers fight over a shovel. One has thrown snow on the other's sidewalk. They slip and fall and slug it out, not laughing yet. The cats and I watch, without taking sides. A new tenant on the top floor next to

Mrs. Ordway's has put a large dieffenbachia in the window, blocking the view into his room, but he peeps around it at me and the cats.

It's two days before I can risk shuffling to the Drive on a cane, and make my way to the oak tree. The titmice and the chickadees eat the seed and shelled nuts out of my hand. A cardinal and his mate appear in the snow, still a startlingly beautiful sight for which I am never fully prepared and which all the starch-sprayed Christmas cards cannot tarnish. They are shy but hungry, and I scrape the snow off the top of the wall and hold back the pigeons till they get the cracked nuts. Stepping high in the snow, the robin, no longer trying to hide, comes for his handout and stays near. I try to tie a can of suet to a limb but cannot reach it. A boy on skis ties it and goes on, pleased. I look the other way when he falls. Dogs pass and turn the snow to saffron. No squirrels today, but I stick around with the robin till the jay shows up to keep him company, then make it to the only bookstall that has braved the cold. Cookie Rothberg has sold her copy of *Lafcadio's Adventures*, or *Les Caves du Vatican*, and on the flyleaf given Gide and me something to think about: "We all screw differently, but falling out of fairies in the Catholic Church is something I can't get excited about." Which cave was she in?

Pard is still not there, but Mr. Gamal has made it out. His coat is getting shabby, but his shoes and his pride are still holding up, also his disdain for old ladies. He does not look at me as we pass.

Nel Thompson, due, has been mugged, but comes out ahead of the game. Besides eighty-five dollars, the mugger took her obituary, which she carries in her wallet as a diabetic carries his insulin warning. A thoughtful fellow, and leaving her unconscious, he sent it to the paper where, accompanied by a purloined death certificate from a previous encounter, it was published, a well-written and surprisingly modest account, with most of the crap near the end.

Taking a tip from her, I have some thoughts to put in my notebook, but soon forget them, as the notebook is still missing. Margarita, when questioned regarding its disappearance, replies only in heated Inca, so I get out my pencil stubs and, using the back of my pigeon feeder, pigeon lover reject ("An old lady's lucky to be recognized by anything"), decide to write about *somebody*—George and his manure trade with the gardeners of East 112th Street.

Allocations were not haphazardly made. Involved was far more than money, and often he sought guidance at the nearby Church of St. Edward the Martyr. Who today? Waiting for a sign, he would sit quietly in the empty little church and close his eyes. Outside he could hear the clop of the horses' hooves as the big beer trucks drew nearer and nearer. Who today? And the church bells would ring out the answer. The fragrance of freshly baked German and Jewish cookies would be right there plain in the beautiful message of the bells, and George, curator of the new-fallen chips, would assign them in his high choirboy chant. "Anoo-other o-one, Mr-rs. Schley-be-ein, one for you-ou to-oo, Mrs. Flu-us-stein."

Of course it helped to have the wind blowing from the right direction, too, says George.

It is now the middle of January, three months and one week since my latest mugging, two months and three weeks till I'm due. Not so the shopping bag woman who, seeking shelter from the cold, is attacked inside the automatic money enclosure at the bank. Her new travel sticker—Come to Sunny San Bernardino—is missing, also sixteen thousand dollars in cash and the old rope she tied around her coat in winter.

Time passes in bunches of weeks. The Huangs, giving up on Martha *and* the toilet, move to Sacramento and leave us their hanging fern and bean sprouts. Sherry, our little friend in Mississippi, becomes thirteen and pines for a pen pal. Shall I tell her of Numero Uno? I think not. Purina replies: No pictures of roaches, either, even if they did crawl inside the camera, die on the lens, and are superimposed on cats' heads.

February wears out. One month till I'm due. In the Biblical Garden of the Cathedral the fig trees are still wrapped like stand-up mummies. But the peacocks are preening under the oleasters and the crocuses are pushing up.

March comes in mild and on sunny days Mr. Loewenstein sits with his nurse on the front steps; he closes his eyes when I pass; the hand-kissing has become too much trouble.

Now and then a bookstall will be open and I go looking. *Science and Society* is there, *Chaos and Night*, *Christ and Culture* are there, but no Pard.

Evelyn goes outside the window to enjoy the sun, and when I spy her is walking on the one-inch-wide railing of the balcony as airily as if she had scaled the World Trade Towers. Her clear intent is to jump across the four feet of empty space to the railing of the living room balcony. From the inside Martha and I freeze, afraid to move or speak. She looks back, sees us, turns around on the railing, and jumps back to the windowsill. Martha puts her paws around Evelyn's neck, licking and cleaning her face for her. Evelyn has a simple look, eyes shut, ears pulled back like a Dürer rabbit's. Soon Martha will sink her teeth into the cleaned place on Evelyn's neck and they'll fight. Perhaps later they'll lie a moment on Sister's bed. Her hand will touch them, but she seldom goes "Ssz ssz" at them anymore.

In the basement Margarita finds a bucket of green paint, almost full and left by the Paysons (key people) who moved to California. Climbing on the ladder and splashing the green over the roach and grease stains, she begins to freshen up our kitchen. Halfway down the wall she quits to go look for super; our toilet is flushing. There's nothing to be done, says super when found: the pressure's just too low. Margarita never gets back to the painting.

Monica's pancreas is acting up and she calls to ask if I will be her next-of-kin. Surely—if I make it through the mugging.

Now it is the first week in March, a month till my Due Date, and I sleep badly, with strange dreams. In one, Monica appears with a funny look on her face: the elevator has made a jarring, unexpected stop and something inside her has snapped; she is thinking of moving to California. In another I am walking on the street and have a feeling that someone is following me. When I turn to see, no one is there.

On Riverside the forsythia is almost popping and on Broadway the magnolias are budding, inferior to their southern kin but still unbelievably beautiful. The winos are out too, earlier and earlier each morning. "Can you spare a dime?" Pinpointing my era, an old one actually asks me this: "Can you help an old man out?"

Celebrating the rites of spring, *all* the toilets in the building are going full flush. In a glorious ode to joy they shoot the works: allegro ma non troppo, un poco maestoso swells to molto vivace, vivace cascades into adagio molto e cantabile, and breaks the jackpot in a pipe-bursting allegro assai.

Every bathroom in the house is under two inches of water.

In the park a nun in flowing garb jogs with two young

boys from her school. The boys are embarrassed, trying to keep up with her, but she is delighted and, holding her arms out in a spirited way, talks animatedly as she runs. From under the billowing black skirt her nylon and suede shoes, dashing blue on white, dart out and scatter the pigeons helter-skelter. This nun's in a hurry. Where is she going? Lots of places. Do they make special running shoes for nuns in a hurry?

With the warmer weather the robin comes onstage only long enough to gobble the cat food and bean sprouts and practice his act. Though fresh worms are wiggling in the walk, his sights are on the camera. Head held within lens range, profiled, high, as in the bird books, he opens with the hop routine—one two three, bob, one two three, bob. Next, front exposure to show the full red (orange) breast and the yellow bill. Silence for this effect, then a rusty run-through on the call notes: "Tut tut, cuk cuk, bup bup," as though he's clearing his craw of the canned goods. After this the caroling song, tentative at first, then swelling gloriously to the acclaim of the crowd: "Cheerily cheer up, cheerily cheer up." Then the finale—the quick, self-effacing bow: It's good to be back, folks—and there is one less worm on the walk.

Easter and Passover draw near, and in a religious mood George calls to remind us that all his childhood jobs had not been in horse manure. On Jewish holidays and Friday evenings work of a more exalted nature had beckoned. Forbidden by religion even to strike the match at those times, Mrs. Flusstein had hired him to light the gas stove. In the spotless kosher kitchen, close by his side lest he set fire to the house as he lit the Sabbath stove (Easy, Georgie, make easy with the match), Mrs. Flusstein, in addition to the five-cent pay, passed cookies. Reaching for the fragrant egg dough stuffed with the succulent prune, George had felt that he was lighting the fires for a better world, for a oneness, a sort of universal experience he found entrancing but hard to explain, and hasn't had since.

"Let there be light," he would chant and, striking the match, hold it high like the Statue of Liberty. In his wheelchair at the Home, he says he now often dreams of it. Passing the cookies, Mrs. Flusstein, no longer afraid he would burn down the house, would call for more. "Make like the Statue again, Georgie. Make like Miss Liberty Bells." He had felt useful and needed then, alive.

Bart Raither and I meet on free blood pressure day at Red Cross. My systolic is higher than his (bad for me), but his diastolic is much higher than mine (worse for him). We part to take our diuretics.

"Water," says Sister plainly one day, looking down from the ceiling. Cora hurriedly fills a glass and brings it. Sister shoves it away. "Aix. A contraction of *aqua.* The French fooled around with the Latin and made it a bastard word. Aix. It means there might be a spring in the vicinity." She looks back to the ceiling as if searching for a further footnote.

The telephone ringing wakes me at night. It is Mr. Loewenstein's nurse. She is alone and thinks he is dying. Will I come down the hall? Watched over by family portraits from the Kiev and Berlin and Paris days, my old friend, the ultimate patrician patriarch, lies in bed and looks like one of the prophets, major, laid out. We watch and wait. His eyelids flutter, he begins to breathe easier, his forehead cools. In each city to which they had fled some of those in the photographs had been killed. Just for living. I kiss my old friend's hand and go. He dies in the morning.

Now it is officially spring and the very First Robin is sighted in the park. But is it really my winter friend, the high stepper, the December deceiver? Who knows? There are three sheepish-looking First Robins lined up on the wall.

"Or a spa," says Sister, getting it off the ceiling.

In the supermarkets now you can buy armloads of daffodils that enhance the heart but last not the night. We fill Sister's room with them. She looks at them sometimes.

It is two weeks till I'm due.

A letter from the Gottchalcks: they just love Petaluma. There's another apartment for rent right near the pool.

Vera, on the fourth floor, is translating Ayn Rand into Serbo-Croatian and reads me some. I work on my income tax. It is not only in dreams now that I feel someone is stalking me.

In the savings bank, crowded, a man breaks through the long waiting line, jumps over the counter, grabs up the money, leaps back over, and disappears. "He should wait his turn like the rest of us," says an old lady.

Cookie Rothberg has sold her Euripides' *Bacchae* to the bookstall and written in the border of page 174: "Cadmus' belief is clearly not wholehearted. He is motivated by fear, family pride, and political shrewdness rather than Truth." Instead of "Aren't we nearly all?" she has written Truth with a capital *T*. Is she quoting her professor or becoming a prig on her own?

Mr. Gamal and I pass near the drugstore. We do not speak. A police car is parked at the corner. He sees it and heads down the side street. The policemen restrain a man who is angrily kicking and shouting at a parking meter. He did *not* park overtime. He watched it. And look at this goddamn ticket on his car. Where is the goddamn meter maid? He'll punch her goddamn nose.

There is still no sign of Pard, but the jolly ginkgo trees are back in leaf, primping and taking mock stances. At the Cathedral a profusion of dignitaries parades in regalia. Unimpressed, a man watches them. "It ain't what's on top," he says. "There's water all under 'em. Goes clear up to Broadway. Gonna wash 'em all away. I been in a boat in it. All the bishops are buried there." He's coming from the AA meeting. I take Sister a leftover palm. She tries to hold it, her hands tremble and let it fall.

A letter from the Huangs; they just love Sacramento. The plants are beautiful and the plumbing controlled.

Eddie Fuller and Fred Freising, his friend, are on vacation in Munich and I go to Eddie's apartment to feed the fish and water the window boxes. The filter is not working and the fish stare out at me, stiff-eyed. Filling and refilling the plastic tube, I try for half an hour to fix it, holding it underwater, keeping out the air. But transferred to its cup, it loses the water, and on the shady side of the street I walk to the pet shop, where a nine-year-old boy waiting to buy a twenty-dollar tropical fish shows me why. Back home I still cannot do it and, disgusted, give up. When I go back later to try again, the welcome gurgle, gurgle sound meets me at the door. It's working.

I open Eddie's big window a little (he's afraid burglars will swing down from the roof again if the window's opened too wide) and pick a bouquet of morning glories and petunias for Sister.

She is too sick to notice them. For now in early April Sister has pneumonia, called by some the friend of the elderly sick. Antibiotics have helped, but Dr. A. on his visit tonight says she will likely die before morning. She is unconscious and, breathing hard, lies with her head tilted back on the pillow. Her nose with a strong Roman thrust points at the ceiling.

Cora looks at me across the bed: she will spend the night. We have run out of Pampers and I use this as an excuse to get away by myself for a moment. "We can make out," says Cora. "She's quit doing." I know, but need the air. "It's too late," says Cora, who does not want to be alone.

"I'll be right back."

13

Huddled in a corner of the elevator, I will it toward the lobby. On the third floor it jerks, pulls up short, then creaks on down. It is only nine o'clock, but the Bulletin Board has a clean sheet for tomorrow. The flushing toilets are already on it, with *Fix that lock*. Do they print the forms up that way, I wonder? The door is wide open and in the growing dark I walk up Broadway to the discount drugstore. It is warm for April and the benches in the middle of the street are full, as are Yum Yum and Baskin-Robbins, the ice cream shops. Tom's, Mama Joy's, and Amy's, all air-conditioned, have lines to the doors. In the drugstore, batches of would-be customers are taking their cool time. The easily concealable stealables, the cosmetic bargains, transistor batteries, and panty hose, are up front, near the eye of the cashier, but the Pampers, that boon to the nurses of the very young and the incontinent old, are high on a shelf at the back. I squeeze past a young man bent over the stationery display and, when a clerk approaches, point.

"What kind?"

"Newborn." They are thin and more pliable, though now to Sister it does not matter what they are. But the clerk, Mr. Gamal, is delighted. He is no longer selling cremation robes for the dying or Falafel for the Faithful, but Pampers for the newborn. This different approach seems to change his outlook on life, or perhaps having a job again has; he is pleasant, almost glib. For coolness I have worn Something Suitable and he notices. "Nice blouse." That he sold me the blouse is mentioned by neither of us. "Nice blouse to welcome new grandson."

I study the showcase of nail polish and think of Sister's hands, shaky with Parkinson's, the nails colored silver by Cora, who cannot clean them for fear of hurting her. Mr. Gamal, short, jumps to reach the Pamper boxes. One tumbles on him and he smiles at me: good joke, fine Arab fellow hit on head by Pampers. He is being extra nice to a new grandmother, like they did in the old country when it was a boy and they allowed the old woman to come and prostrate herself, bowing. "Okay. Nice grandson, huh?"

It would not hurt me to smile back—old ladies should smile back, grateful for any smile they get—but I cannot, and inspect Dr. Scholl's remedies for ailing feet. Hammer Toe, Toe Flex, Arch Support. Not a Tamarind or Toe Tie in the bunch. No knee pads, either. Yesterday Sister, while her bedsores were being powdered, had fallen on her knees to the floor. "Come, up, up, darling," said Cora. Arms and legs helpless, mouth open, teeth out, Sister looked up from the floor with scared, pleading eyes. "Sister." I reached down to help; she tried to catch my hand, like the sick ones in paintings or films who know they will be left behind on the prairie while the wagon trains go on westward. "Up, up, darling," said Cora, then lifted her bodily back into bed.

"First grandson, huh?"

I follow Mr. Gamal sullenly to the cash register. He hands me the three-fifty change from my five-dollar bill. "Okay? Good luck to new grandson."

"Grand*daughter*," I almost shout.

I have upset myself foolishly, been needlessly impolite (isn't it always needlessly?), and, trying to compose myself before going back, walk on up the street under the sidewalk roofing to spend a few minutes at the bookstalls. The old standbys are here, but after a practiced scan, in the dim light from the store window I find a paperback copy of *Roderick Hudson,* long out of stock. I pounce on it to read to Sister when she's better. *The Ambassadors* is her favorite James, but this has good print, a Sargent watercolor, "In a Medici Villa," on the cover, the characteristically charming preface by the author, and the usual excellent introduction by Leon Edel, his editor and biographer; $1.57 with tax is the bargain price: $1.93 the amount of my take-home change.

Momentarily cheered, and to avoid as much of the roofing as possible, I decide at the next side street to walk home by Riverside Drive—territory off bounds after dark to all except the quick stabbers, the foolhardy, and those lucky enough to live there. But tonight I am homesick for the distant past and this is a street well known to me, a puffer to walk up, a breeze to go down, and I now turn west on it toward the Drive.

But even the buildings on this street have not escaped the cellblock framework of the iron bars. The skeleton frames, jointed like old Erector or Tinkertoy sets, shroud the façades, danger signs warn of entryways, wooden roofs barely height high darken the sidewalks. An occasional flash of a car's lights brightens eerily the tomblike gloom.

But in spite of the obstacles, or perhaps because of them, intrepid tenants have found a way to defeat them and, crouched on the stoops, peer out portrait-like through the iron frames. Some drink from beer cans or from brown paper bags. Others lick at ice cream cones. Too many have brought their hi-fis. Several hope I have a nice night.

Few pass me, choosing to walk on the opposite side of the street where only a scattering of the buildings, sturdier or unornamented, have the covering. But I am headed for something, a memory or whatever, to help Sister and me make it through the night, and I pick my way on past the obstructions. In the middle of the block I finally see light. A parking lot has been squeezed into the vacated area between two encased buildings. Fenced in, unattended, it threatens by lighted sign to tow away all illegal parkers.

Years ago a clubhouse for young women had been here. Recitals were held in its parlors with southern tea and polite clapping. Pure and/or musical were the qualifications for residence, and more southern girls than are on record had hit New York either one way or the other then, sometimes both. Sister was not *musical*, that I can vouch for, and in 1927 had spent the night here when she and Polly, a sorority sister, on their way from Dallas to Convention (they never said "the"—just "Convention") had driven a Model A Ford two thousand miles in only seven days, a First that local Texas papers were quick to equate with Lindbergh's feat of the same May.

A car wishing to park honks and edges nearer my kneecaps. I back up and wait. And now just ahead is what I have come to see—jacked for the demolition claw, lights busted, windows out, beat up and vandalized, but still standing in there taking it, and making that statement (good-bye) as boldly as any other old reject. This is the apartment house where with my mother we'd first lived, teenaged and fresh off a five days' Gulf voyage from Galveston. Here my mother said for the first time but soon learned not to say at all, "Where I come from we don't do it that way" (drop in to visit via the dumbwaiter shaft). In a raffle run by the building's elevator operator, Johnny Cheeseborough, Sister had won her first and only turkey and was never again to win anything comparable except a copy of *I Promessi Sposi* in her Italian class.

In the basement Tailor and Cleaning Shop, now dark and abandoned, worked Jackson, who pressed my brother's courting pants every day at 6 P.M. for a quarter and was the first black man of my own age to call me "hon." A lot of firsts, a long time ago, I think, and have to reach up and smash away the tears.

The car parks. I have seen what I came to see. So go home, jackass, while you're still in one piece. But the trees on the Drive invite me on. This morning, bird-feeding, I had found a beautiful leaf, placed in the path like a gift, for Sister. Acknowledged idiot, I go on now and under the streetlight stoop to pick up a new pencil someone has dropped. The next moment my hand is jerked behind me and I am thrown down the short flight of stairs into the basement areaway of the old building.

14

Though due, even overdue, I cannot believe what the pain in my ribs screams is all too true.

"Why do you *do* this?" I manage to gasp. "*You?*"

He looks down at me, smiling a little. "Mama, I thought you done learned in Mugging Class not to recognize nobody. I'm sorry you done it." He is leaning against the banister, one foot propped against the steps. In the faint light under the stairs he even looks a little sorry. "You miss old Pard, then, Mom?"

I do not answer and he sits down by me on the steps. "I sorry to be late for our appointment but I Head Man in my organization and I been away finalizing some schedule changes." His legs are long and he is proud of them. One stretches out shorter than the other, and this fact he tries to hide by bending over to examine his shoes. A glob of greasy black dirt from the areaway sticks to the sole of one. "Goddamn filth, get off my good jumping shoes." For an instant as he wipes his shoe on the edge of the steps his back is to me. I try to rise. One of his shoelaces is loose; he tightens it, tests it, and ties again, then holds the foot out for inspection. The shoe fits high up on his foot as though for support; the laces are long and fall over the sides of his shoe. I inch up farther. He does not bother to raise his head.

"I trust you ain't planning no miraculous getaway up the stairs there while we having our little getting-to-know-you-better scene." He examines the other shoe. I am almost to the top step. "I don't believe in them fast hits—maim, grab, run. I warm 'em up first, just to give 'em a idea what they're in for. Like this."

Moving quickly, he pushes me back down the cement steps. Instinctively I cry for help. Under the streetlight I see the feet of a couple who pause on the way to Broadway, used to, but refusing to accept, the evidence of their ears. Perhaps it's a dog howling. Bound to be a dog. The shoes start up the hill. Yes, but what kind of dog that goes like a old lady screaming in an abandoned building? Any kind. Hurry up.

My friend, who has stayed behind me in the shadows, pulls a bottle from the pocket of his slacks.

"Sorry I had to show you that, Mom, but they're not gonna help you, even if they wanted to. That's the awful part of it. That's one reason I keep at this, just hoping someday somebody *will* stop." He takes a long drink and puts the bottle between us on the step. "I'd offer you some of this rotgut, Mom, but I know it ain't your brand, and I need it all, anyway. Here, though." He reaches in his pocket again. "Try one of these little whistles I give to all the old people to call help. Blow it, ain't nobody gonna pay any attention to it. They think it's part of the usual night noises or just another old kook getting it in the gloaming."

Trying to crouch back in the dark out of his reach, I blow—a weak sputter. He shakes his head. "You just like the rest of 'em. When they need to blow, most of 'em are so scared or twisted up funny where they fell, they can't make no sound on it, just a whimper. But nobody but me would come if they heard it. That's who you up against, them, not me. I'm just a helpless little old minority. Me and you both, Mom, just two innocent victims on the opposing side of the grab bag. So relax here with old Pard and get that idea of help out of your head. My next appointment ain't till ten-thirty and I done picked this place special so me and you can talk without no disturbance. Believe me, ain't nobody gonna stop *nowhere*, but they sure ain't gonna stop here.

"Now excuse me a minute while I set here loose and meditate. Anything out of the ordinary you hear, that's my mantra clanking."

I lie scrunched against the wall and wait. Sister, Sister, Sister. He sits with his head down and breathes deeply. He has on slacks, T-shirt, and canvas shoes. If he has any weapon, except himself, it is not visible. After a couple of minutes I feel his eyes studying me.

"Sorry to conk out like that on you, but I been picking up little books all day and giving out them whistles to old people. What do you think makes people so mean, Mom, they don't try to help each other out like I do with the whistles and the little books?"

Scared and hurting, I have no answer. Just as well—he has a prepared statement on the tip of his tongue.

"Of course you understand I *always* been nice to old ladies, but I kind of a late bloomer in the children's book racket. 'Late bloomer, hell,' people say. 'You're sick, man. Go to one of them children's books shrinks and get yourself straightened out. If you want to make it with one of them little mousies in a bonnet or one of them little choo-choo trains, let it hang out. Or buy yourself some of them goddamn little children's books you keep yakking about, and stuff 'em, man!'

"Buy 'em, I say, why I got to *buy* 'em? They're mine already. I'm twenty-two years old, Mom, too old to get a job, but I ain't going on welfare, even if that money do belong to me. You know that, don't you, that all government money belongs to the people and people is *me*. So it belongs to me without me working for it. You agree with me, don't you, that what's yours and the government's is mine?"

I'd be a fool not to, and nod. Sister, Sister.

"So the same way your money's mine, I figure all the little children's books belong to me, too. But I didn't have no politics to back up the claim down home where I needed 'em. When I was a child we lived in this country town and we didn't *have* no little books, no big ones either. We had the schoolbooks they hand out ever' year, of course. *The Brave Little Bedbug with VD, The Leaf That Spits at Old Ladies, Pussy for Kids,* all like that, but I wanted one of those little *outside* books so bad. One somebody had picked out for me special, like a gift, not through no goddamn school system or the library where the lady says, 'Now, don't get no grease on this nice little book, John Howard Haines. Be careful where you set it down. Don't crumple none of them nice little stiff pages. I want you to grow up and be a fi-ine reader, John Howard, to learn not to say "with you and I," get your "only" in the right place, and be a credit to your race!' Je-sus God!"

Laughing, he reaches for the bottle. "But I learned that be-a-credit-to-your-own-race crap later. We didn't have no library in the nigger part of town."

"We didn't have any at all," I hear myself say. "But we weren't thugs."

He takes a drink from the bottle and looks at me, interested. "Where'd you pick up your little personal books, then, Mom?"

"At the drugstore."

"Hell, we was so poor we couldn't even *go* to the drugstore. But I used to slip into the white section of town where all them bugheaded little bastards sitting on the front steps, piss-eyed, reading these little children's books somebody had gave 'em. Got big painted pictures on the backs of cats, or mice, a little deer with a crocheted hat on, or an old hen with biddies riding on a merry-go-round.

"I'd hide there in the bushes, watching, envying them kids, wishing so bad for one of them books. Them kids sit there on them nice strong steps with a good straight banister so's they don't fall off and hurt their little selves, just sit there reading these children's books in their laps. Sometimes their mama bring out lemonade and tea cakes, but them kids don't even raise their eyes to eat. They don't even thank their mama. Now and then they turn a page or change the position in their laps. People passing say, 'Look at them adorable children, reading them children's books. Ain't that the sweetest picture? I wish I had it right on my wall. Honey,' they call, 'what's the name of your book, precious?'

"But them stuck-up little shits don't even look up when people speak to 'em. They just read on. One day, though, while I watching from the bushes, this boy setting there holds up the book for them to read the name. I can see that name just as plain now, Mom, as I see you. Remember I just seven years old then, but I gonna die with that name in my head. *Mr. Pard and the Grasshopper King.*

"But you know what that little boy doing back of that book, Mama, pretending he reading so hard? He playing with his peter."

15

While he talks I keep trying to inch down the steps away from him. Below us is an alleyway that connects with the next street. There is light at the end and shadowy figures passing. My hope now is to get within calling distance.

"Ain't that disgusting? When he goes in the house a minute and leaves the book on the steps, man, I run out of them bushes and stole me a real special book, for me only, Mom."

I crawl too quickly, he shoves me down. "Lay still. You know I ain't gonna let you sneak up that alley. There might be a mean old bugger bear up there that mugs you. Don't even give you no little whistle to blow." He pauses, as if an unbearable thought has struck him. "I ain't by any chance boring you, am I, Mom?"

I shake my head.

"Then take it easy. I know your back hurting you some there, and I sorry about that. Don't speak if it pains you, just kind of nod stiff, yessir, yessir, when you approve. Being the Head, I quite capable of carrying on a long-winded conversation with myself. Where I been I ain't had somebody to talk to in some while. You talk to somebody that ain't a Head, then they think *you* ain't the Head. So when I with all them non-Heads I just grunt. You realize me and you ain't had a chance to set down and talk together yet, Mom, just indulge in the waving act? Well, I aiming to make up for it tonight. I gonna prop you up nice here on the steps and shoot us some real old-timey breeze.

"Because now though I got the little book I didn't have

no place to read it, because we didn't have no steps on our house even as good as these. They live nice down there now, all right, man. They think people crazy to stay here in New York when they could be jiving it up down there—walk-in closets, stereo in the can. But history recounts it ain't always been that way, and my papa never *did* make it big.

"You remember the Depression, Mom? Before my time, but my papa was too poor to get *in* it, much less ever get out of it. He brought the Depression papers up to the courthouse to qualify and a big shot there from the committee say, 'No sir, we ain't gonna be dragged down no lower than we already are. We got *some* standards, man.'

"Wouldn't even nobody from the North come down and take their pictures, Mom, like Lowest Poverty Group. They say, 'Of course we willing to talk the South down any chance we get,' but we too low for even that. Wouldn't nobody believe it, they say, and it'd ruin their selling chance on the next bunch of pictures somewhere else.

"So Papa was so poor when he built the house he had run out of wood by the time he got to the porch and he put it up to Mama: You rather have a roof over the kitchen or porch steps on the front? Old Mom took the roof because she spent all day working in the field, nothing overhead, so when she come *home* to work *inside* she want to be *under* something. By the time Papa got able to get more wood to build the porch ever'body had got used to the status quo and didn't want it. The house was built on stilts, and they liked the privacy, besides it gave you a way to kind of look down on people that was outside looking up. That was about the only way we had to feel higher than somebody else, Mom. And for us kids it became a game. We could just jump out the door into the yard. Some of the old folks broke their legs a lot before we put a old mattress there to break the fall, but to us kids it was easy.

"We'd get us a good start in the back of the kitchen, race up the dog run, and see how far we could jump out the front door. Of course we didn't have the proper special shoes for the jumping like we do now." He stretches his legs out for me to admire the shoes. I give them the steady stare of approval and he goes on. "We was barefooted. You remember a fellow named High Streak, Mom? Tall, skinny boy with a mouth full of teeth that held up his fist in the picture? He's my cousin that went to the big-time long jump on that training we had. We'd put corncobs out in the yard to measure the distances. High Streak could jump to the Number 16 corncob way out by the well, but I couldn't get past the Number 2 right by the footpath. Maybe you ain't noticed, but I have this slight defect in my foot, kind of hold me back behind the others. They were all ahead of me, then, the big, far jumpers. Poor little old crip always a little left out there, Mom.

"I'd get so lonesome for something, just any little old something, it didn't have to be big, or alive, just something to hold on to, to cut the lonesome. I'd get me one of them big oak leaves like Sister likes and I'd say, Man, I'm gonna hold on to this leaf this time, and ain't nobody gonna get ahead of me on the leaf. That's a promise, I'd tell the leaf.

"But it would dry up or the other kids would snatch it. Then I'd find me a little baby rabbit and say, I'm gonna believe in this little rabbit to the day I die. But the old dog would catch it, or somebody would run the rake through it. Once I kept a hen egg for a long time, kept it a secret, slept with it, and hugged it, and finally crushed it. So I found out the little storybooks was the only thing I could hold and keep, 'cause I put 'em in my head. Most times I made up my own stories. I heard one of them fast talkers on TV once, what they call a social worker, say she thought not having no hot water or no papa at home made many children grow up to be criminals. I add to that that it's not having no little children's books. You might say the lack of steps didn't bother us because we turned the lack into an asset, and now I'm ahead of all the jumpers. I'm the Head Man. When you're that, all you got to believe in is yourself. You are It.

"But back then, without no steps, I had to take old *Mr. Pard and the Grasshopper King* and read it on the johnny hole, with a old rooster that hung out there and zapped the hens when they strolled by. That's where the boy owner and his mama found me. 'There's that little old nigger boy been watching me through the bushes,' he say. 'What's he doing messing around with my nice little children's book, setting out there? He crimping my nice little stiff pages. Look at them funny toes on his foot, Mama. They turned backwards. And what that old rooster doing like that for, Mama?' We couldn't afford no rooster knockers, Mom.

"But my own old mama whammed the daylights out of me and I didn't get to keep that book after all. But it started me on my career and now I have a nice collection of children's books at my place. Some of 'em first editions, priced high, and some just have sentimental value. Of course, I didn't *buy* 'em all. I stole most of 'em. The way I work it so the bookstall people don't get suspicious, I always openly buy one, and steal three.

"I wouldn't call it exactly stealing, though, because books are the enrichers of life—it's printed on the tote bag—and the enrichers of life should be free. And as you say, Mom, they rightfully mine anyway. And in a way I pay for 'em, too. You realize, don't you, I have to hire these boys to turn over the stalls so I can zoom by like the Head Man enricher and pick up the books. You can't pay 'em just a dollar anymore; the price of grass has gone up.

"So they far from free, Mom, but I'll never forget that first one I stole all by myself. The story is that Mr. Pard, who in real life is the Frog Queen, goes out to find the Grasshopper King to get the secret of how he makes the long hop. Mr. Pard runs a racetrack in the backyard of the pool where it's dried up, and the grasshoppers has been outjumping the frogs lately and ever'body's complaining they been losing money on what they thought was the sure bets. Not only that, the grasshoppers have been nicking up the backboards of the pool real ugly. So Mr. Pard cons a grasshopper girl to let him in on how they do it.

"Get a load of what this fresh chick hoppy tells him, Mom. It seems that grasshoppers have got a long thing attached to the end of their stomach called a ovipositor. That's what the girl *said.* It means it lets the eggs out. Well, grasshoppers are experts in letting out the eggs, so they done made a little gum scum that sticks to the pool and slows up the frogs, and where they been pushing hard against the side of the pool to get a good start on the race they done gummed it up more than was allowed. But it worked out fair to ever'body in the end—the frogs ate the grasshoppers, then jumped, so they *all* won the race.

"But you know I ain't never seen that little book nowhere." He pauses a moment, watching me. "You believe all that stuff, Mom?"

"Why not? Tell me your name and address and if I ever run across it I'll send it to you."

He laughs at this one, almost choking on his drink. "With the cops, too, huh? That's real cute, Mom, but I ain't *that* dumb." He grabs at the bag and jerks out the purchases. "What's the name of the book you bought off that stall? Pampers. Pampi be a good name for a little children's book, kind of a takeoff on old *Bambi.*" He throws back the Pampers box and holds up the book. "What this *Roderick Hudson* con all about?" In the light of the street-lamp he gets the plot off the wrapper, then reads aloud from the Preface.

"'At the same time I did so helplessly and consciously beg a thousand questions. What I clung to as my principles of simplification was the precious truth that I was dealing, after all, essentially with an Action, and that no action, further, was ever made historically vivid without a certain factitious compactness though this logic indeed opened up horizons and abysses of its own. But into these we must plunge on some other occasion.'"

Disbelief, wonder, scornful admiration for the gall and the gas, leave him speechless. Henry James has muzzled him—for a moment. When he speaks again his voice is strained and muted. "I'm gonna give you first shot at that, Mom. What the hell does that dude mean?"

He looks down at me, waiting. I am imprisoned against the steps, my back hurt, my ears bombarded. I try to think of what Sister under the circumstances might answer (This is ridiculous?) or Cookie Rothberg, who had written in the margin of *The Beast in the Jungle* "He doesn't know what she's talking about and she doesn't know what he's referring to." The jagged railing of the steps sticks in my ribs. I'm trapped with a compulsive talker-mugger who could turn ugly again. My spirit is bruised, my whole self affronted, and I am very angry.

"He means shoot all muggers, you big-mouthed thug."

"*Me* big-mouthed, *after that?*" He rejects this at once. "Ain't no use to call names now, Mom. That sounds too negative. I see it this way. Old Pard here, of the Horizons, has come across something about the Grasshopper King of the Abysses, been cheating on the game. They belong to these two rival hockey teams. Somebody been slipping somebody a mickey, and old Rod done rush out away from his mama and got his horns busted. But it says here we gonna work it out at some future date. All the questions are up for grabs. Don't ever give up. I known as a idealist, of course, but that's what I get out of it."

Somewhere in the neighborhood a clock dongs ten.

"But like old Henry says, Mom, we'll plunge into this on some other occasion. I ain't gonna bore you no more. I got to go now and lay the scene for my appointment with your sweet-potato pal. Give me your money."

"You've got your shoe on it."

He moves his fine footgear, blows off a speck of dirt, and I take the crumpled dollar bill and the ninety-three cents out of my blouse pocket. He gazes at it silently a moment, then grabs it and pulls at my pocket. "Now where your real money at, that you carry for muggers? I saw you with that five dollars at the drugstore. I know you got more because your social just came a few days ago and didn't nobody break the box. Not that you get much, I'm sorry to say, because I need it. Good thing Sister Keith gets the six hundred dollars. The Ninety-sixth Street boys call her Kip or Kate, but I say, No, it's Keith from her great-grandmama that was captured by them mean old Indians when she was a little golden-haired girl down in Dixie."

I know better. God. I know what I'm in for. But I have to ask. Swallowing hard, I get it out: "*What* Ninety-sixth Street boys?"

16

I watch him sit back down. "Got you that time, didn't I, Mom?

"You know what we do down on Ninety-sixth this time of the month? We get out in the middle of the street and drink a extra shot to good old Social. It do you good to see it.

"All over the city the Oldie Goldies is getting their Security. You one of the few holding out, Mama, not having it sent direct to the bank. That's something I want to talk to you about. I want you to do like the fellow says and send it. That way we can depend on it being there. It's just like we have our own bank account. Some old people that get their checks at home fool around with 'em, stick 'em under a pile of leeks or sweet potatoes, and don't get 'em to the bank for days. That ruins our bookkeeping.

"Sent direct to the bank we don't have that trouble. We know where the cash is and can figure out our budget. We'd rather have the cash any day, Mom, than have to break open the mailboxes, steal the checks, and pay some low-down cambiamos crook to cash it. When you see us on Ninety-sixth Street we ain't playing dominoes or checkers or Little Bird in My Cup out there in the sunshine on them benches, and at them tables we put up. We're putting together torn-up or canceled checks. You tear up a bank statement with all the canceled checks, we find it, and piece the signature together. You can't tear 'em up too fine for us. We gonna get that signature pieced together if we ruin our eyes and break our backs. That's what they call the Work Ethic, Mom. And like you old ladies say, it's a pain in the butt.

"But all we got to do when the check's sent direct to the bank is take the cash from some poor old scared lady or man on the way back home. Of course, they've thought up some funny places to hide it, and I ain't going into the gruesome details, but the minute we get rough they just go flop, flop and hand it over. Some just hold it out like they handing out leaflets: Vote for Old Ladies. I mean we can count on that, Mom, just like we can count on ain't nobody gonna stop to help 'em. So quit trying to flag somebody down and listen to what I tell you. Ever'body got a right to be able to *count* on something without the human factor bugging it up. That's the reason we put in these Central Files." He takes a drink and waits.

"My God," I say.

"How else you think we operate a big deal like this? We have these secret agents in each house on each street. We learned it from the government. You'd be surprised the people anxious to get into that kind of work. Makes 'em feel important, the way you feel on your first stickup—you scared to death but it gives you a feeling of power, too. Like that first little book I stole—I felt good and I felt bad, too. I even throwed up a little bit right there in the johnny, with the rooster. After that it was just Go get it, it's yours. Ain't nobody gonna be able to push you around no more. That's all we after, Mom, plain old FOC—freedom of choice to be the pusher and not the pushee.

"And we usually get away with it, too, because we got plenty of help. There's people in your house, Mom, you wouldn't dream of that turn in information for our files. People you say good morning to, or hold the elevator for, if it happens to be running that day. The informer sends his information to Central Files, currently located in one of the side-street hotels. But don't look for us there. We change the location ever' week, and the Head Filer. Sometimes we work out of the post office, change the box ever' week. Sometimes we use the old comfort station.

"At the Center the Head Filer gives you the name of four or five old ladies or men due for a hit, you get the résumé on 'em, see if their credit's good, and decide which one you want.

"But it's more than that, Mom. We're like a little close-knit family there, like a co-op company. The workers own the stock and run the business. No bosses except one, and no union. Some of us is black, some white. But we all just as equal and individual as can be—within the framework of the organization, of course. We all have our jobs to do, we all pool the profits. We got to. Ain't nobody allowed to leave there without being searched. I ain't gonna get the Achievement Award tonight either for this dollar ninety-three.

"And that's something else I want to talk to you about—quit giving away our hard-earned money to that redheaded beggar. Sure, we let him clean up in the bathing place we rigged up in the comfort station, but why ain't he out working like the rest of us? We ain't holding out *our* hands begging. We even put in our own night school to learn our trade better. Sometimes we take brushup courses at the New School. Meet some nice old women there."

He takes a drink and looks at me, waiting. I look back and he goes on.

"And what *is* the position of women in your club? you ask. Well, the position of women in our club is that they ain't got no position in our club. They got their own setup. We ain't the only group of crooks working out of Ninety-sixth Street."

He moves his foot closer, ready to slam it in my face. "Ain't you gonna ask me *how* the group works, Mom?"

I make him wait—but not for long. "How does the group work?"

"*Our* group works it this way. After we get the info from Central Files we fan out into certain territories, regulated by the census, like the congressmen. The census is falling off, though. Lot of old folks have died one way or another. But not by nobody in the Social Club. We don't kill. Maim a little, maybe, if they don't give up right off, but we need you alive. Truth is, we the best crime fighters in the city. We got a patrol that don't allow no butting in from outsiders. In fact, we as good at keeping old people alive as the doctors, and for the same unselfish reason—a stiff don't draw no more social or Medicare. Of course, there's some cheats that keeps them checks coming long after putrification, but that's the exception. We anxious to save the old folks. We need your money as much as you do, and being government money it belongs to us as much as it do to you. Don't it, Mom?"

The foot moves toward me.

"Glunk."

"Keep it clean there, Mom, and listen to how the old folks is dying out, in spite of they supposed to be living longer. Food so high some ain't eating proper, or they so nervous about being robbed they don't go out for it. So we have a little Outreach Program where we give 'em free meals. We also have a door-to-door Escort Service so they can get outside safely. Even with that, though, two of the census districts have had to be combined and reorganized. But I happy to report the personnel of our organization has remained of the same high quality."

He pauses for a drink, then, jabbing the shoe at me, says, "It's your cue now, Mom, to inquire about the high quality of the personnel."

"How about the high quality of the personnel?" I inquire.

17

"Our personnel is real high-class stuff, Mom.

"First, there's Ern, he's our Intercom Man, only he calls it Non-Com because he can blow that thing out in a minute. Except sometimes he likes to play around with it, falsifying his voice. 'Mail man. Delivery. B. Altman's,' he'll call through the bell, and half the fools in the building will open up for him. He studied electrics in reform-vocation school, so he's had the advantage of an education, as they say. You don't have to be *un*educated to be a crook, Mom. Naturally Ern's our Elevator Man, too. When somebody's stuck in the elevator, that's Ern wielding his mighty power. He's got the tip of one finger missing where some old lady got him, but he ain't bragging how it happened, and it don't interfere none with his light touch and delicate approach.

"You know all them times Martha and Ev raise up like they hear something in the hall and you say, 'Set down, you don't hear nothing.' Well, they *do* hear something, Mom. That's Ern pussyfooting it around looking for a door to open. Getting around the way he do, Ern's a natural for our Bulletin Board and No Heat and Hot Water Man. He's a sure bet for our Meter Man, too—Parking and Electric. He can outcon Con Edison on them electric meters. He don't take much to plain mugging, but we're behind schedule and he's got your pal Mrs. Reeder tonight.

"Hubie, he's our Schedule Man. Takes his job real serious. Steals these bought printed slips and sends out notices to victims like a dentist do. 'It has now been six months since your last appointment. Please call my secretary and make an appointment as soon as possible. Your continued good health, and all that shit, depends on your prompt reply.' Sometimes even if the people ain't nowhere near due, and he's made a haul on a new batch of notices, he'll send 'em out anyway, just to worry 'em, like he done you. Calls it psychology. Then he sends a second notice—'Busy, busy, busy, aren't we all? We all need reminders, don't we? Your health'—and he goes on like that. Sometimes he prints the second notice himself, learned it in calligraphy class.

"It ain't no secret, Mom, why we schedule our muggings at least six months apart. It's so the victims have time to collect enough money to make the job worthwhile, and get a little careless. Like even when you knew you were due, you came prissing down this dark street by yourself, just asking for it, right to this empty house. I was watching you after you left the bookstalls, and kept hoping you would, and hoping you wouldn't, too. You know how dangerous it is with all these SROs and Mentals around.

"After Hubie, there's Beck. He's our Telephone Call Man, our MIT Man. All them calls you get when the fellow hangs up the minute you answer, that's Beck. Quick-handed, he can get the receiver back down a half second before you get yours off the hook, so he don't have to pay but you can hear him. Cheaters like you and your neighbor Monica do that as signals, but Beck does it to limber you up after the overdue notice. People with unlisted numbers think they're safe. 'Oh, I just couldn't get along without my unlisted number,' they say. Well, they ain't *got* no unlisted number, Mom, because Beck's figured out the mathematical probability (he calls it the *im*probability) of every unlisted number there is and lists 'em in all the bus stop shelters with all the lost dogs, Commies' meetings, and apartment hunters. 'Do you want $500 absolutely free?' he writes. 'Then call me at this number night and day.'

"How does he do it? You know the way they figure out street numbers, what side street a given address is close to? You take the address, cancel the last figure, divide by two, add or subtract the key number—sixteen, eighteen, twelve —and maybe you get within two blocks of it. Well, Beck does it kind of the same way. Only he uses how many letters in the man's name, divides by two, then for the key number uses the first two figures on the ninth race final. If it's a odd day of the month he subtracts it, if it's even he adds it.

"But if he don't even know the name and is just trying to pick an unlisted number out of the cold, he adds up a whole block of *listed* numbers, say six, takes the third figure out of each one, adds the day's quote on the last race, looks across the street to see what time it is on the big clock, subtracts that from the temperature—Celsius, Mom, we big on Celsius—then halves the whole thing, and one sixth of that is the unlisted number. Took him some time to come up with the idea, and there ain't many that understand it, or go along with it. First time he done it a woman answered say, 'What took you so long to figure it out, Sick Stick?'

"Beck's our Computer Data Man, too. You realize we couldn't keep all our records without the computer, don't you? Beck rigged a typewriter to the telephone and wired a connection to the subway and we get free electricity for our computer, courtesy of the third rail of the MTA. People complain of bad subway service. Part of that's old Beck.

"You with me on this, Mom? Do it sound good to you?"

I nod my head, the required answer, and he talks on and on, shooting his breeze. Headlights shine briefly as cars come down the hill, and in the added light I watch his face. I watch his hands. I watch the T-shirt—good old Pard. The bag falls from the bottle as he drinks and I watch the liquor go down. I watch the legs passing me by on the sidewalk. But I always come back to the shoes. Blue on darker blue, with the curved toe, the white laces, the cushioned ankle collar, they seem no different from the ones that jog past me on the Drive. One is kept pointed directly at me and I make out the number on the sole—132. What does it mean, I wonder, and move my hand slowly toward the bottle.

"It means these shoes is a numbered edition for poor little old crips like me, that's all; they make 'em for slaphappy nuns, too. So get your hand back there and quit trying to hit me on the head with that bottle. Or I gonna shove old 132 right through you. Set there and listen, because I gonna talk about the Mouse Man, Eustace, now. He can plant them little mousies around in the halls and the lobbies and the drain while you still laying it on to the super. He's got a training school where he learns 'em to swim fancy. It ain't necessary, and it ain't connected with the job or anything, he just likes to do it. His real work, though, is Mail Box Breaker and Toilet-flushing Man. He can stand down at the club and make them toilets start flushing all over town. Sounds beautiful, like a symphony. Beethoven Ninth, Mom.

"Whitcomb's our Garbage Inspector Man. He can size up garbage with a glance, even without the handy electric see-through device he can tell if there's anything we can use in the files, like torn-up canceled checks or old magazines with your name and address on 'em. He's our Scatter Man, too. Scatters things around for old ladies to find, little pieces of wood, just right, pencil stubs, even leaves, Mom. It's Whitcomb, not the mighty oak, that sticks them leaves under the tree just before you get there. Sometimes he hides birds, too.

"Remember that wok you got, and that cocktail cart? Whitcomb put 'em in the basement for old Margarita to find. He even found your notebook she threw away in a pile of papers. We all read it with great interest. We think you should put your crap nearer the beginning, though, Mom, not the end. How you know people gonna stay with you that long?

"Garfield's our Filter Man. He can tippytoe into a room and fix or unfix a filter without you or the fish ever suspecting he been there. I don't mean just fish tanks, either. He can syphon gas out of your tank while he's carrying on a conversation with you about the high price of gasoline. He's a good man with motors, too. Him and Maccy Ventura, our Explosives Expert, work together. If we need a job done quick, they blow it up with the hard stuff. Trouble is, Maccy kind of a double-crosser, a commuter type, lives out with the Queens crooks. We had to put a tail on him to see if he's selling us out to another club.

"Then there's Dr. H.J., our Stand Up Jesus and Obit Man. When sorrow strikes, or trouble hits the family, and the loved ones don't know how to take care of the money, Honey Jesus reads about it in the paper and comes right around to comfort 'em. Look out for him, Mom, he's a live wire. Yale Man and highly educated, *he* say. He's our You Know, You Know Man. He won't let nobody say it. Says it's stupid and shows lack of vocabulary, like overuse of obscenity. Ever' time we say 'you know' more than six times in a minute, put the 'only' in the wrong direction, say 'with you and I,' or add the 'very' to 'unique,' he gives us a hard time. Between him and Townsend, our Black English Man, I don't know half the time whether to say 'I have, I has, I am, I be's,' or what.

"But Dr. H.J. a far thinker. He got big plans for our neighborhood. Gonna put us on the map. He ain't only Advance Man for the *Second* Coming, he pushing for the Third and the Fourth, and the World Without End Amen one. Inflation, Mom. With the machinery set up and the overdue notices printed, why waste 'em?

"If anything happen to me—I say *if* because I a young man, of course, but any business where a bunch of thieves is involved is risky, Mom—*if* it do, I'd like for Dr. H.J. to take over for me. As I say, I'm Head and the Number One Backup Man. Even if we is, be, or are all equal, we know there's got to be a Head somewhere. Ain't nobody that equal. If somebody gets throwed in the pokey for some time, or don't catch on to the job quick enough, ever'body say 'Get the Backup Man, get the Head here. He can do it.' They mean me. Then Dr. H.J. backs *me* up when I have to be away for a while supervising or setting up a new district program.

"That's why I'm here with you now, Mom, this is part of my new territory. Our schedule ain't quite settled yet, the reason I ain't been around lately. But I picked you for tonight, freedom of choice, and done my homework in Central Files. I don't bother to cut that children's books and poor-childhood shit with ever'body, or making the interesting little side remarks on Celsius.

"I even reserved this place for us, bring back the old memories to you. Of course, I would have did it anywhere, but I'm like Nelson, our Rape Man. He don't just grab any chick or old lady and do it. He got high standards. He picks out one and follows her for days, finds out what she likes, what she eats and reads, do she belong to the Philharmonic, if she's well thought of in the community. If she don't have no nice mantra or litters the street, or do she talk ugly or got bad breath, he don't fuck with her. He starts a study on somebody else.

"Don't worry, though, Mom, you ain't in his district and rape ain't my bag. But you know what I bet? I could walk you home up the street, across Broadway, walk in the lobby where Ern's broke the lock for me, go up in the elevator he got running, twist off them three locks of yours, push away the security desk, knock you in the head with that big flashlight, steal me a Nieman Marcus brassiere, get your social out of the top dresser drawer behind 'Saga of a Sauce,' the rejections for the cat piece, the pigeon piece, the roach piece, Mrs. Schleybein, the old one from H. L. Mencken, get me a butcher knife, a quart of Jim Beam, a bowl of keys, and ain't *nobody* on the street or in the house gonna try to stop me. And ain't that the goddamndest biggest shame—"

Before I can speak he shoves me back into the shadows. Somebody has stopped.

18

Mr. Gamal has stopped.

"Everything okay?"

John Howard gives him a long stare before answering. "Sure. Old mom here just sipped a bit too much celebrating old times." He holds up the empty bottle. Even on a step below him, John Howard is a head taller than Mr. Gamal.

"How come you think everything ain't okay, Shorty Pop?"

Mr. Gamal ignores the threatening tone and comes closer. John Howard stands in front of him, trying to hide me. I make a vast effort to raise myself so Mr. Gamal can see the blouse. Pushing up with the Pampers, I half make it.

"Celebrating new grandson, huh?" Mr. Gamal recognizes me and understands.

"Let her lie flat," he says. "Use the box of Pampers to prop her head." And he smiles, as though remembering. It was the way they did it in the old country when they brought out the bubbly and Granny overcelebrated the birth of a new grandson. Turning the chips toward Mecca, they had piled them high for Granny then, and now, as if in fun, Mr. Gamal lifts a merry, imaginative glass. Over the brim his dark eyes seem to be telling me something. And I remember the Petroleum Club and Geoffrey's essay: *Moslems do not drink. Temperance, along with the Islamic purdah, is a strict religious law.* What laid out old Granny when the grandson was born was not liquor but tripping over the veil when she washed all those diapers.

"Okay?"

Mr. Gamal waits for my answer.

"Okay," I say, and he starts down the hill. He is in no hurry, and once he looks back and raises the glass again. When he goes on, John Howard lowers himself to the steps, limp. "Why the hell did he stop?"

"He's not afraid of you." Neither am I. Now.

"He's a fool."

"But he stopped." Mr. Gamal stopped. I sit up a little, freeing an arm.

"He don't know the customs. It's against the computer. Computers ain't equipped to take an exception like that."

"*Yours* isn't." Bending, I pull the bag closer. "You said *nobody* would stop."

"He *ain't* nobody. He's a little drugstore A-rab that sneaked into the house I live in while I was away supervising. He ain't gonna live there long, either, because I'm gonna slap the Good Samaritan medal on him for stopping.

"And don't you get in the act again, or I'll come get old Ev and drown her under that faucet where she contemplating the flow of water. If Ern's cut off the water that day I'll throw her and Martha out the window. Damn disgusting spoiled cats. I've throwed quite a few out the window. Ain't a one of 'em ever landed on their feet, either. They ain't no better at it than old ladies."

It happens so quickly we are both surprised. Henry James catches him in the head; the Pampers fall flat. John Howard stares at me a moment with almost a hurt look, then hands me back the Pampers.

"I ain't no roach, you know, Mom. You got to practice that phony sidewinder aim a little more. Like this."

I try to shield my face as he throws me hard against the railing and I fall back on the steps.

"I'm gonna keep old *Roderick* here for my collection. You take the Pampers for Sister, but the bet in the club has odds ten to one she won't last through the night. And now I'm gonna give you one last reminder not to get fresh with the Head no more."

I see the lifted foot coming toward me and push the Pampers in front of my stomach. Pliable, for my new grandson, they are also thin, and the shoe catches me in the ribs. The last thing I see before I lose consciousness is number 132 coming at me. When I open my eyes the Head Man is looking down at me from the top of the steps.

"Sorry I had to do that, but I'm the Head and I got to be in charge. Now I got to go and apologize to the sweet-potato kook, but watch out on that airplane. Russell, our Turbulence Man, says there might be trouble." A shoelace has loosened in the kick and he stoops to retie it. "Promise me you'll carry that little whistle in your purse always. If you get in trouble, just blow and I'll come. If I ain't in residence the informer'll pass the message on to me."

When I'm able to crawl up the steps and start up the hill, he is nowhere in sight. The people sitting in front of the houses watch me. Through the iron frames they look out like judges. One or two snicker—an old shopping bag woman who's had too much. No one offers to help. On Broadway people pass me with their ice cream or frozen yogurt cones. They lick high into the soft mounds, pointing their tongues up.

The drugstore is closed. So is the Registrar. Holding in my cries, I walk on. All along the street people smile and say, Take care, have a nice night. The radios play loudly. The door is still unlocked and I enter the lobby.

On the Bulletin Board under the flushing-toilets sign a note has been tacked to a big leaf. *Have faith,* it says. *You will never be alone with me and Jesus.* I stick the leaf and the note in the bag with the Pampers. The elevator rises slowly to the seventh floor. Cora meets me at the door.

"You better hurry."

19

Can you describe him?

No.

Could you identify him if you ever saw him again?

Yes.

Would you be willing to come to the station to do so?

Of course. He is a self-attested thief, a son of a bitch who kicks old ladies when they're down, and throws cats out the window. And I can't get him off my mind.

After Detective Pickens and his companion from the Twenty-fourth Precinct go, Cora straps my ribs and we sit with Sister. Holding her hands through the night, we watch her leave us. At seven she seems to quit breathing, but for an hour we cannot tell whether she is dead or not. Her eyes are open, seeming to follow us as we move about the room; we see a pulse, we think, a heartbeat, we hope.

Lu, a long-time friend, arrives to be with us. At eight I call Dr. A., who comes at once. Mind gone, limbs paralyzed, Sister saves me the agonizing decision of filling or not filling the antibiotic prescription that might, or might not, prolong her life. Sister has died of pneumonia and, though surrounded by friends, alone.

In another hour Mr. Sheldon, the undertaker, follows Dr. A., collects the death certificate, and we write the fine-print obit and make the grim arrangements. Sister and I have long ago agreed on cremation, and the family plot in Texas for interment. Cora helps me choose one of the Christmas robes for the cremation, as we no longer consider the other suitable after its ordeal in the dirt last night.

The one we choose is simple and cotton, though Cora would wish something finer for her lady. Hoping to add tone, we attach the Phi Beta Kappa key, but it falls off and I decide to carry it in my purse as remembrance.

Mr. Sheldon asks us not to watch as he takes Sister out of the apartment. Cora, in tears, goes to the kitchen to phone in her numbers bet—the date of Sister's death. In the window of my room the finches are singing. I listen and watch the little red heads bobbing till Mr. Sheldon appears below and slides Sister into the back of the hearse. A neighborhood group has gathered in front of the Christian Science Church. The hearse is double-parked, but out of respect the honking does not start at once. A garbage truck grinds once, then the sanitation men stand by their black bags and do not heave. A moving van waits patiently; a sofa bed comes out in pretty good shape; the drivers stop it in midair, a kind of salute. Large Louie, resting on a stoop across the street, rises and tips his big cap. The upstairs soprano hits a high, almost conclusive note.

After the hearse turns at the Cathedral and disappears down Amsterdam, I sit alone a moment in the living room. Sister, Sister, Sister. The cats, cowards, come out from under the sofa. I try to cry, get a hard, dry run, then notify publicity at the college, and they call the *Times*. When George calls he has already guessed the sad news. Poor Keith, my darling, he says, and please bring him a picture of the grave.

As though looking for a review of a favorite book, I turn next morning to the obit page and look for word of Sister. Handley Belkin, who wrote the lyrics of "Getcha, Gotcha," and Roger Rankin, an old outfielder of the American League, are remembered in a few informative lines. Lydia L. Collins, socialite and philanthropist, patron of the Opera Guild, gets a much bigger spread with a 1943 portrait in her Red Cross uniform. Masucci Ventura, killed instantly when the starter in his car blew up, and alleged to be a victim of interfamilial differences, is dismissed at the bottom of the opposite page, with a picture of his tree-lined street in a quiet residential section of Queens. Last to see him alive were his six-year-old daughter, waiting at the window to wave at him, and his German shepherd, who had followed him to the end of the walk. The car, a 1978 Mark IV, presumably a mess, is not shown.

Sister gets a good review. After the listing of biographical facts and the modest professional accomplishments and honors, a colleague, quoted, calls her "quick to translate the ideal into the practical—a five-foot-two tower of strength." Sister would have liked that.

Now people begin to call. Thank God, they say, comforting, Sister is at rest. Her long trip is over. Many come with food from the Hunan Garden or Mama Joy's. I spend the morning dumping the cats out of the suitcase, trying to pack, and talking on the phone. Reservations with Delta assured, Harris, our steadfast Texas friend who will conduct the service, arranges with the local funeral parlor a day and hour—two days hence, 2 P.M.—for the service and gives them a biographical notice for the paper. Is it beautiful there, he asks, as it is here? Yes, but warm for April.

It is afternoon before I can get to the drugstore. Mr. Gamal has called in sick. No, the Hispanic owners do not know his present address. Nor, it seems, could they care less. They do not even glance up at me. At the fruit stand I wait by the sweet potatoes, but Bart Raither does not appear. The clerk shrugs when I inquire, and when too many people pause to speak of Sister, I go home and call Bart on the phone. He is indisposed.

Later in the afternoon Detective Pickens telephones. They have staked out plainclothesmen at all the bookstores with stalls and have picked up a suspect who they think fits my description of the perpetrator. Will I come to the station and see if it is he? No, they have no reports on Mrs. Reeder and Bart Raither.

At the station I look in the cage at the man standing under the bright light. He cannot see me. The officer on duty tells me the circumstances of the arrest. The prisoner had come to the stall to read a book he said he had no money to buy. *Seven Types of Ambiguity*. My God, I think and look at him closer, do they read that anymore? Was he planning to read it standing up? Was it the book nearest for him to grab, or did he actually choose it, to "read classy" on the bus? When the clerk apprehended him, book in pocket, he said he was a poor student and could not afford it. But he had a .32 pistol on him when arrested, and was wanted for three robberies. Of the same kind of book? I wonder and think, Give him the book. *Seven Types of Ambiguity* is many things, but a children's book it's not. And the man in the cage is not Pard.

Am I glad? I don't know. Later I walk in the park, trying to decide. The bluejay flies down from the oak and sits on the wall to be by me, or so I wish to believe. On the walk I find a dead warbler, cut down in April flight. Or was it planted here by Whitcomb, the Scatter Man? My ribs are hurting and I go back to Broadway to look for Mrs. Reeder. The shopping bag woman is near the bank sporting a new travel sticker, but I fail to see Mrs. Reeder and at the store Dominic in vegetables says she has not been in. And look at all these leeks he's got left. I take the bus to Ninety-sixth Street, past the side-street houses with the artisans crouched under the cornices and the gargoyles hanging over the roofs, past the set-back entrances and the flower boxes under the canopies. Somewhere here is there this intricate network of crooks, dedicated, hardworking specialists in crime? Or did one psychopathic, schizophrenic, brain-arrested, compulsive-talking long jumper think it all up?

If the latter, how does he know all these things about our house and the people in it? He doesn't, I tell myself, it's an old building (this he *could* know) subject to the ailments that happen to most old buildings and old people. He listens on the street, too. Couldn't any assiduous listener have learned the things he knows? But could anyone who talks as much as he does listen that much, too? And who but me knows about my rejection slip from H. L. Mencken? Could he have got it all out of the notebook he claims Whitcomb, his Garbage Inspector Man, found in the basement? True, Nel Thompson when she called about Sister managed to sneak in "Got your piece about old George back yet?" But even she could not guess that this morning I found "The Saga of a Sauce" shoved in the drawer back of Mencken and "Another One, Mrs. Schleybein," where Pard said it was.

But wasn't he making it all up?

Absolutely, says Detective Pickens. He got the Central Files idea from a stationery store advertising one. We've been over the territory inch by inch, building by building. All we've found, besides good, law-abiding citizens, are the usual winos, junkies, pimps, prostitutes, panhandlers, purse snatchers, petty thieves, forgers, and hit men you'd find anywhere. All working independently. All we need now is to find out where the perpetrator lives. And we will.

I know who knows where he lives. Do I speak?

No.

Otherwise the place is clean as a whistle, says the detective.

Yes, but what kind of a whistle, I wonder. An old-lady whistle? I walk down the street, looking. A block fair is in progress, the chipped china and the family photos begging to go back home. A street player fiddles on a violin; Celsius is up, sweet potatoes are down, the community garden is a huge, boarded-up hole. Some harmless-looking derelicts are drinking beer and laughing on the benches; a few chary walkers like myself steer clear of them.

"Will you buy me a cup of coffee?"

I had not seen him till he spoke, and now light into him. "No, indeed. Nor a hot dog, nor a doughnut. Why don't you get a job like everybody else who works hard? Do you think because it's people's money that it belongs to you? And did it ever remotely occur to you to say please?"

Immediately ashamed, I offer two quarters. The man refuses them.

"I never beg," he says. "I have some pride, you know."

"Where do you wear it?" I ask angrily and watch him walk off. He wears it in his shoes, in the long way he walks on paper soles for a bath; he wears it in the triumph of cool superiority over those who stoop to give him money, or slip to the other side of the street to avoid doing so.

When he moves I see he has been standing in front of the stationery store.

The phone is ringing as I enter the apartment. "Who was the first and what was the last?" asks someone. I know by now it is not Gertrude Stein or an indecent phone caller, but the wrong number, someone from a bar wanting to know the winner of the ninth race. I hang up and, holding the cats at bay with the sidesaddle, pull out the Books in Print. Heavy, unwieldy to hold, but a fine cat stopper, it contains over 538,000 titles currently available. *Mr. Pard and the Grasshopper King*, if it ever was, is not now present, but *Seven Types of Ambiguity* is listed in both hard cover and paperback.

Early the next morning, as promised, Mr. Sheldon, a

good man in a very competitive business, sends the ashes by messenger. He has warned me that the package may ring at the airport security gate, and with the cats waiting to pounce on the wrapping paper, I open the very ordinary-looking three-pound package to see why. It is no alabaster vase here, for sure, nor one of Mr. Felkin's recycled pickle jars, but a tin container that Sister would call a half-gallon syrup bucket, and of which she, a great lover of ribbon cane, would have approved. I look at it wonderingly a moment. *Sister?* How could you box up Sister in three pounds of ashes and tin?

Then, as Martha claws at the paper, I hastily rewrap the can so Cora, who would want it to be gold at least, cannot see it, fold the brown paper ends under, secure them with the masking tape, and put it on the desk with the other packages.

Promising to return (as soon as I can), I hug the cats for the last time, and Cora, who "doesn't like good-byes," disappears to call in her number; having failed on Sister's death date, she decides to play 132 from the jumping shoes. At the door I take in another package from the postman, add it to the undelivered pile on the desk, and go back to answer the phone. It is Detective Pickens: Please leave him the telephone number where he can reach me in Texas. They have an important new lead.

A Mr. Gamal has come forward with information. He knows where the perpetrator lives. An illegal alien, Mr. Gamal is now under house arrest.

I give him my cousin's number, put the little box in Channel Thirteen, and go to the lobby. People in the house have gathered at the front door to see us off. And this is the time I should cry, then think that, having heard of my experience night before last, or seen the police car, those present are merely worried about their keys. Is the informer among them? I wonder, and assure them that Cora, who is staying with the cats, is thoroughly reliable and will probably be scared to leave the apartment at all, much less ever think of using their keys.

But they don't mean this at all; they are our friends and have come to let us know it. "Come back now," they say. "We'll be thinking of you." Some have brought little presents—books, candy, Toe Ties. "Don't let 'em keep you down there." "I won't, I won't." "Take care and come back soon." "I will. Thank you, thank you."

Eddie Fuller, who has returned from vacation, is driving us to LaGuardia. Though he does drink beer as he drives, but not in the city, Eddie is an expert chauffeur and Sister would like it, going in his shiny Chrysler. On the way he plays soft music of her vintage. He has gone to the trouble to load the cassette player—"Ja-da," "Three o'Clock in the Morning," "Tripoli." We sample the liqueur chocolates Fred Freising has sent and talk of Sister, of the fine people in the house, of Harlem, which we pass through to reach the Triborough Bridge, of Munich, where they call him "Der Schwartze," of his own sister in North Carolina who sends him the bacon, of filters (I'm the best filter fixer he's ever had), and of disco, which is badly cutting into his jobs. I hold Channel Thirteen on the seat between us and gratefully agree to call him to meet me on my return trip.

At the airport security gate the tin box rings and we have to go back. I can imagine Sister's pleasure (her last ring, loud and clear) and produce the covering letter from Mr. Sheldon explaining the contents of the tin box. We pass through again. The bell rings. Hating to go, Sister must have her hand on the button. Examination of my purse unearths the tin whistle, and the third try allows me to pass through. On the plane I take a seat by the window. Get an extra seat, people said, put Sister on the seat by you. You're entitled, you're escorting the body. And remember the broken ribs. But I had made my reservation late, the plane was booked solidly for a convention in Washington, and I leave Channel Thirteen between my feet where I can watch it.

My seatmate places his carry bag, a squat, shiny leather affair bulging like Picasso's goat, under his aisle seat. We adjust the seat belts, get the smooth assurance from the cockpit (Thanks for flying with us today, friends), have the cheery demonstration, learn where to puke and how to breathe, and take off. I wait for the sure crash. Sister always pretended to like flying—how else could she get to an Aix?—but I'm frankly scared stiff and only do it for funerals. My fear verges on the sick, admittedly. Why could it make any possible difference to anyone but me for a little old insignificant woman like me to die? Because I'm carrying the ashes, that's why, it wouldn't look so good. Besides, I'm entitled. There're other reasons too.

Cora will adopt the cats, but how about Estelle, Joan, and Linda, my handicapped light globe friends from Torch, who will ring and ring and ring and I will not be in the bathtub to go answer? (Can they really hear the tap turn on?) And who will feed the birds and the squirrels, who kindly allow me into their lives for a moment but who don't need me half as much as I need them? A lot of people. Who will be next of kin to those in need? Anybody.

Lucky this time, we clear the whole runway. I always wish the trip were over while we're still on the runway, and sometimes it is. That poor pilot in the cockpit of the 1914 plane *looked* like I always feel—desperate. But today we ascend, and as we get higher and higher and head for Washington I look out and see the jigsaw puzzles appear on the land, configurations almost Etruscan, strangely archaic Greek vase affairs. Warily entranced, and to help my ribs, I pull down my little table, order J.D. for me and a double for Sister; Jim at home, Jack in the air. The prompt arrival of this warming draft lulls me into the false view that flying is not all that bad really and that the clouds are just perfectly beautiful. A lot of fine, important people fly every day, finer and more important people than me. I look down through the clouds to the hard, far earth and try to think of a few FIPs more important and finer than me, and crazy enough to do it every day.

Is my seatmate one? Is that the reason he is leaning forward, looking across me out the window, scared to death? Not so; I now see the tag on his lapel says "MLA," not "FIP." Book-oriented, I at once guess Modern Language Association. Convention. There'll be a lot of Robert Penn Warrens and Allen Tates and Fugitive/Agrarians there. Is that the reason he is scowling so, appears so nervous? He is a very serious-looking fellow, impressive, though under high tension.

Is he looking for a job, as half his convention fellows probably are? Has his college knifed him, even with tenure and a sure grasp of sixteenth-century English prosody and a little thing coming out next month in the quarterly that very few of his colleagues will bother to read? And what of his colleagues? Did none of them stand up for him? (Smile.) Where were the rest of his department? Probably canned and on the same plane, too; it is full of astringent, competitive-looking males.

He leans closer, as though seeking a way out. Is he as scared as I am? And what *is* that tremendous object hovering out the window now, getting nearer and nearer? Another plane? We look at each other and panic. No, it's a wing. It's been there all the time. Give her a wing, they say, scare the hell out of her. The *Fasten your seat belts* sign flashes on. (I never *un*fasten mine.)

"It's not dangerous, though," I hear my seatmate say. He has an accent, like Dominic in vegetables at the store. It would have to be Italian prosody. "It's just that the plane is tilted."

The plane is *tilted?* My God, the plane is tilted, the sky is falling, and here I am way up here with a desperate Italian fellow without a job.

We pass out of the clouds and the plane levels. The seat belt sign goes off.

I breathe easier and consider passing Fred Freising's chocolates to my unemployed seatmate, who probably hasn't eaten in some while, but after a quick count refrain out of rank penury. Instead I finish my drink, thinking. Central Files indeed. I had seen it in the stationery store, too, a real dandy file case, with lower, middle, and upper filing facilities, fine storage for résumés, six-months notices, and signature forgeries. A handsome pure steel addition to any social club. A real Central File.

Maybe. But suppose Detective Pickens was wrong. How about all those derelicts down at Ninety-sixth Street that I've seen trying to piece those signatures together? The whole idea of an informer in the house is silly, granted, but who could it be? The one that occurs to me is Mr. Huang, who had got so angry with Martha about the bean sprouts and the fern. A person who will lose control of himself over a couple of bean sprouts is not stable. Oriental, too, you know. Not to mention that continuous toilet sending secrets down the drain to Eustace, the Flushing Man, on the other end.

Up here, 36,000 feet, out of touch, on a limb, responsible to no one, you can believe anything, or nothing. I give the scenery another glance. If we *are* flying that high—that smooth-talking cookie driving just announced it—why are those clouds out there by that second wing coming up like this, instead of going down like that? Do they know something I don't?

I finish my drink and am about to start on Sister's when the *Fasten your seat belts* sign flashes on again. God speaks from the cockpit: "Just relax, friends. We may experience a mild turbulence ahead. Nothing to worry about." Our plane immediately swerves to the right, stands us on our heads, upsets my little table, cracks a couple more ribs, and rolls the contents out of Channel Thirteen. Hitting the high places, the plane balks, then steadies. Groping at my feet, I push the box back in the bag and for a moment play feelsy with my seatmate, also groping. His hands are smooth and furtive, almost as though rubber-gloved or tenderized. A womanizer, I bet, getting away with murder, feeling around on whatever he can. Doles out his grades according to skin texture he gets to feel. Mine does not pass the test, for he suddenly jerks his hand back, snaps his bag to, mops his pants, plainly blames the upset on me, not Russell, the Turbulence Man, and at Washington departs with his overstuffed briefcase, as do many others.

When no one gets on to take the empty seat, Sister and I travel the rest of our journey side by side, almost in peace.

Central Files enters my mind only once more: what about those checks the bank insists have my signature when I know they don't? And as for the informer, how about those Cuban actors on the third floor that speak all that Spanish, for goodness' sakes, and give those plays by Oscar Wilde? That's pretty damn suspicious, ain't it? And the Mad Scientist? They say he is working on cell experimentation that would mature human young as early as animals. Three years and they would be on their own, even more than they are now. They say there are funny little things walking around in his apartment; Margarita vows she's seen one in the basement but hasn't yet been able to bring one up to us.

And while we're on the subject, how about old Cookie Rothberg with all her wisecracking comments on better writers than she could ever hope to be? What secret code are they? Or don't forget Bart Raither with all that sweet-potato bunk, who's he contacting with that scale? How about that high diastolic? And all that hot air about giving away his gloves? He never gave away anything in his life except those rotten potatoes. Or Mrs. Reeder with her leeks; when she picks them up, doesn't she cross them in a funny way before she puts them in the bag? And how about that shopping bag woman? Do she and Mrs. Reeder meet in that automatic money place in the bank and swap information? Is that why she changes her travel stickers so often? And the redheaded beggar with his no "please" act? How about Mrs. Ordway hanging out the window all the time waving at people? And that tenant across the street hiding behind that dieffenbachia and using those binoculars to spy on old women and cats? Or is he watching all those little people in the scientist's apartment on the floor below us?

And while we're at it, think about Monica a minute—sure she lets the cats call, but she hasn't got any plants and how do we know that's a genuine mousetrap she wears up there? She's pretty careful not to show it to anybody. Why? Because it's a recording device like the spies use. She's from Canada, you know. And about Eddie Fuller, don't leave him out. He's black, too, like Pard, isn't he? If they're not out killing one another, you know how they stick together. And those songs he played on the ride—wasn't there a kind of communist beat to "Melancholy Baby"?

And old Kirby, bouncing around with all that goodwill showing—popping by the lobby to give Sister's name the final mispronunciation—wasn't it bourbon from his store Sister was drinking when she fell? And where was he the other night when I needed him? Closed.

And how about that damn jay that's been bugging me all these years? And that four-flusher with the First Robin routine, for Christ's sake?

Or is it some washed-up old bishop operating out of that canal under the Cathedral?

I think of various things away up here—of Margarita and her gifts from the basement, of Vera translating Ayn Rand into Serbo-Croatian. I ponder Beck's method of obtaining unlisted telephone numbers—if it's so infallible, why, when I tried to get super's unlisted number, did I get a recording—"We've been unable to complete your call as dialed; please check your number and dial again"?

And if my seatmate was so upset when he left the plane, why did he say to me, almost apologetically, "I thought I touched a mouse?"

But most of all I think of Mr. Gamal, who had stopped.

20

Die in April if you can in East Texas. Or die in April in East Texas if you can. But do it, if you can, for it is incredibly beautiful and you will hate to leave it but it is lovely for those who journey from afar to see that you do. Though they have been planted along its highways, this is not native bluebonnet or paintbrush country, but that of the wild white violet, yellow jessamine, and magnolia that tie the tongue with their presence and fragrance. This is piny-woods country, scent country, and in my sister-in-law's Chevrolet we travel from Houston to our old hometown, Claire, now transformed by oil and dams into the millionaires' town.

Entering, we pass by my grandfather's place. Our gingerbreaded and many-porched old house has been replaced by a low-slung, elegant brick. Boxwood, not tamarind, is the showpiece here, and I wonder if Miss Roxie, reading as I did that its wood is prized for making mallets, has toppled the tamarind as she did the flagpole. Sandy Creek has long gone down the drain; where Sue taught us to dodge garter snakes and swan-dive from a tree limb, there is a tiled pool with Olympic board. We pass a parking lot for a washateria—gone, too, the old black washpots. We drive on through the rich overgrown town I no longer know my way around in, past handsome homes, many designed by my brother, who was never to own one. They have changed the directions on me, too; North, South, East, and West as I knew them are now fused into connecting superhighways. It is only when we pass the courthouse and the jail, on which my grandfather's little store had fronted, that I get my bearings, immediately to lose them: the drugstore where I exchanged empty medicine bottles for my little personal books has become the local TV station.

The car trip has not been kind to my broken ribs, and in my cousin's home where even the roaches are air-conditioned, where the toilets give a polite flush, say "Come again, hon," and quit, where no one hangs "shits" in the window, and where they still call me "Little Ruth" (my mother was "Miss" or "Big"), I retire early. Taking off my dress and my slip, I lie down in just my strapped ribs. I have a room to myself—as do Sue and my sister-in-law and my niece—a whole bed, a shade that needs no props, a TV, a bowl of sweet peas, and a plate of divinity candy. The windows, closed for the air conditioner, face on the back garden, and outside one a chinaberry tree, with what seems overdoing it a trifle, has a mockingbird on call.

It is the guest room for family, formerly the headquarters of Little Hugh, now aged forty-five and a district judge in Houston, as his father had been. A repository of his youth, it contains stacks of old *National Geographics*, bound copies of *Nature, Birds, Defenders of Wildlife*, a bicycle, and a needlepoint rocker no cat claws have ever touched. Hugh, a member of the high school football team, had embroidered it himself. Not the heftiest or the fastest, he had spent a lot of time on the bench and, now on it again, wins prizes in Houston needlepoint circles.

It is a library of sorts, too. No Trophy Room here, as in another cousin's home. Ardent advocate of conservation, Hugh Junior has brought up his children with the same belief, and mixed in with the Save Our Earth and Protect Our National Forests publications, three generations of children's books stand out. Old friends, *Twenty Thousand Leagues Under the Sea, Huckleberry Finn, Robinson Cru-*

soe, Treasure Island, Tom Sawyer, Tom Swift (this has got to be Hugh Senior's), are here. Others are unfamiliar to me —*The Ski Plane Boys, The Soccer Kid, The Hardy Boys.* Then, looking over the bowl of sweet peas, to me the most nostalgic and fragrant of all flowers anywhere, I almost fall out of the feather bed.

Up to now the only other books I've ever stolen were Joe DiMaggio on baseball, a paperback from the Columbia NYPL branch, just sitting up there on the counter for grabs, and *Gammer Gurton's Needle,* far inferior to Joe and available in many anthologies, but imperative at one time for some reason now inconsequential and unremembered.

I pull it from the shelf—Out of Print in the BIP but very much In, here among Hugh Junior's environmental books.

On the wrapper, Mr. Pard, though appearing sly-eyed and slack-jawed, looks to be of stronger mettle than Roderick Hudson, not a fellow who would make just one fine sculpture, sputter, and give out. But the pond with the racetrack in the background, done in dullish green and badly nicked with grasshopper hooves and ovipositors, could not stand up to Sargent's Medici Villa. And who is the author? Mr. Pard. Biographical in form but full of memories and self-disclosures, it begins: "From the very first minute he went to the Organization Meeting he knew—"

My cousin knocks on the door. "Are you all right?" I reach for my robe and put the book next to Sister in Channel Thirteen.

Shall I tell my cousin I took it? She would gladly give it, but what reason could I offer for wanting it? A thief of my acquaintance who has this lovable, sentimental streak in him needs it for his stolen collection? He belongs to this club of thugs that preys on old people and I want to reward him? They already think people who live in New York instead of here are dotty, and some are. When they visit New York they stay in friends' apartments on Park Avenue and consume high cuisine in the same territory. Most have never been to the West Side, except on safari to Lincoln Center.

I call out to her that I'm fine but in bed, and respecting my obvious need for privacy, she wishes me pleasant dreams and goes to receive another donated funeral meat. In a sudden surge of loneliness I take out Sister, unwrap the package, and look at the box.

It looks tin, all right, but it's not the one Mr. Sheldon gave me. No half-gallon here. This is a gallon, no desiccated little old librarian is in here. This is an ornate box, silver, in simple bad taste. Where I had made a botch of the package, hurrying to rewrap it before Cora saw it, this is done with flourish and skill. Professional, yes, but executed with individual care by someone keenly interested. On top of the box is printed in Gothic letters: M. Ventura. I look closer. Are those asterisks after the *M* and the A small diamonds or bad punctuation?

For a moment I'm too stupefied even to turn off the TV. Had I picked up the wrong package on the desk by the door? I remember placing Sister's box there so I would not forget it, the object of the journey. On the way out to the elevator, when I hurried back to answer the phone, had I been so surprised it was Detective Pickens and not my handicapped girl from Torch that I'd mixed them up? No, the only other package there had been from Neiman Marcus, and even N.M. doesn't wrap 'em up like this till Christmas. This had come from the plane. Was my seatmate carrying M. Ventura's ashes to the *Convention?* Were they trying to get *ashes* a job? Or was he killing two birds with one stone—"Wait for the Convention. You're entitled"?

I doubt it. And do Italians have ashes? They have large, costly coffins with bodyguards. But only a few, and only in the movies. I now remember M. Ventura's obit in the *Times*. There is very little left to make anything but ashes out of when you've been blown to smithereens starting your car. But suppose these are not ashes at all. And of course MLA does not stand for Modern Language Association, which does not meet in April but late in the year when you've already seen the leaves fall and will take any job you can get. What MLA member could afford this send-off, this sumptuous little home away from home, or would choose it even if he could? If they *are* ashes, are they "hot"? Had the Ninety-sixth Street gang stolen the remains from the morgue and fixed them to ruin identification, and for what possible motive? Was my seatmate ordered to get rid of them, had he planned to palm them off on me all along, not knowing he would get Sister's in return and be where he started, with a bunch of alien ashes on his hands?

Had he thought he was going to be able to throw them out the window, for goodness' sakes, did he actually think, as I used to, that you could open the window and, like the man in cockpit in 1914, just throw? Why did he not flush them down the toilet? Had he been afraid, again like me, to lock himself in the spooky little john, even for the amenities? Had he, as a last resort, ordered the turbulence from Russell? Had he Mickey Finned the Jack Daniel's so I would not notice when he switched the ashes? Why go to all this convoluted trouble? Why had he not just checked the ashes at the airport, or left them on the subway where, according to a news report, eighteen urns, ashes intact, were found last year? Or, if he wished to play it romantic, riding a ferry, fed them to the gulls while he recited "Sunset and evening star," as some of my lying acquaintances relate doing?

Shall I call my cousin back and declare the whole thing off? She has piercing, determined eyes and the look in them would be flinty: Are you crazy? And leave me with all these meat loaves? All afternoon they have been coming in, one apiece for everybody, with the fried chicken, baked ham, and quichey dishes from the *Junior League Cookbook*. Even in the unusual spring heat they have done this for us; are those fancy microwave ovens they all use air-conditioned? What shall I do? Shall I doom Sister and M. Ventura to ceaseless transidentity, or shall I make it a life quest to go from city to city (on a bus) seeking out Sister's true ashes? "And wear a black veil and my Phi Beta Kappa key you've got there in your purse while you're doing it?" I hear Sister say. "Certainly not. Don't be a jackass. Do what you have to do."

I reach for the last of the divinity and hear the announcer on the TV. "The funeral of Keith Reed will be held tomorrow at twelve and not at two as incorrectly reported in the press. I repeat, the funeral of Keith Reed will be held at twelve tomorrow at Glenndale Funeral Parlor. Interment will follow at City Cemetery. Friends of the family are invited." In thirty minutes I hear it again, every hour on the half hour, too. Though Harris and I had both verified the time, somebody at the paper had goofed and the funeral parlor is making them pay.

There's got to be a funeral, all right, but whose? I turn off the TV, take the Phi Beta Kappa key from my purse, and paste it over the name with one of Hugh Junior's conservationist decals. *Extinct Is Forever—Save Our Rare Species* is too much; I opt for a plain flying bird. Then, tired, unbelieving, I lie down again. It is a fine bed, I can stretch full length with my feet spread out, my arms flung. No cats. The percale is silken and kind to my broken ribs. The sweet peas are fragrant. But sleep does not come. I open Mr. Pard, published by the Concerned Press in 1967. Calling it a children's story is like calling *The Pupil* a story for schoolboys, or *Animal Farm* a book about pigs.

MR. PARD AND THE GRASSHOPPER KING

From the very first minute he went to the Organization Meeting he knew this one was different. Something about the whole setup made him think so—the hush in the weeds, the respectful way the wind held down the rustle, pulling it in at the sides, the way the sun kind of shone on just him, like a spotlight, the way a shoot from the green reed bent over to shade him, the way the others, usually so noisy and busy, stayed so quiet, not moving. Even the tadpoles were still. Playing it modest, he stayed at the back of the pond and kept his eyes on the bottom mud, squushing it up around his webs.

"Now here's the way it's gonna be run," he heard somebody say, somebody that grunted way down in his throat and was bound to be the Head Shot who decided things.

"Garfield, you gonna be the Informer and the Filter Frog.

"Russell, you the Turbulence Frog.

"Beck, you the Contact and the Computer Frog.

"Hubert, you Personnel and Public Relations. You send out the overdue notices.

"And Pard." Now when he heard his name he stiffened and slipped a little in the mud. Nobody seemed to notice and he wiped the dirt off his webs; one way he held them they looked like fine jumping shoes.

"Pard, you gonna be the Book Man and the Backup Frog. Anything anybody else can't do, I know you can do it. Come on up nearer the front, man, where you belong." Moving up nearer to the front now, he bumped his head on the log. But nobody laughed, like they had the time his foot had caught on the root and he had fallen face down in the slime.

"When I ain't present, you is the Head Man. The Big Jumper."

Though he had dreamed of it, of course, he had never been the Head before, only the little Next-to and Here-boy, here-boy-you-way-in-the-back-there. Sometimes he had trouble deciding exactly who he was—a great big fellow up front like he knew he really was, or the little one that stayed in the back behind the others and threw out the tin cans and the cigarette stubs.

But this man meant *Head*. Some of the others were smarter than he was, he knew. Eustace was quicker with teaching the mouse to swim, Beck was better with electrics and phone numbers, Whitcomb was the garbage expert, and Ern was the top elevator man. They would put up a fight. But where were they? Hiding to pounce on him, but he would beat them all. He could jump the farthest, even with the little broke web. He knew he could. He puffed up some, saying it, and his new T-shirt stretched big across his chest. And now he spread out and in one big jump he made it easy to the front.

"I mean you are In Charge, man. You gonna make this place clean and healthy."

He looked around to see how the others took it.

Then he remembered he was the only one left in the pond—he thought.

21

The next morning before the service Harris, Sue, and I take the little box to the funeral parlor. The rugs are thick, the sofa deep, the art inexcusable, the secretary helpful, and the young director seemingly amiable. Though he has been our friend and confidant since childhood, I do not tell Harris of the true identity of the ashes (if indeed I know); he and his wife, one of our fonder kin, have lovingly prepared a eulogy not to be spoiled. Sue, when told, tries to look shocked, then we giggle, and face our sad chore: arranging a simple monument to be erected when the earth settles.

A variety of choices for the inscription comes to mind: "This is ridiculous—in my opinion," "*Again?*," "Quo animo?," "Certainly not," "It's a bad arrangement," "Had I the choice." Sue, quicker than I, suggests "How long within this wood intend you stay?," one of Sister's single-liners from *Midsummer Night's Dream,* or some of her French throw-aways, "Pas encore," "N'existe pas." We are not being frivolous, or disrespectful of the dead, we are merely trying to keep Sister with us as long as we can. All the suggestions seem suitable for her, but except for "Andante ma non troppo" from her Philharmonic days, what of M. Ventura? He has some rights; after all he is here and Sister is where. We settle for the name and date (Sister's) in Roman numerals and put a spray of the sweet peas on the box. Money changes hands; the service can begin.

The free publicity on TV has paid off and the air-conditioned chapel is full. Nel Thompson must be advised: setting a date is of prime importance, but the free exposure on the air is no drawback, either. Our dear cousin Ross, subject to blackouts and donor of all those big Heritage Club books in the fireplace, plus rose hips in abundance, sits by Sue and me.

The pianist begins the service with bits of Mozart and Schubert, then works into "Ein' Feste Burg." On cue, Harris rises and speaks impressively of Sister's life and work, hard to do with someone who was no big shot, had no children, did not drive a Red Cross ambulance in World War I or II, or had not been a patroness of the Opera Guild. With no panoply of family or fame to hitch on to, he quotes from her own sayings. "'I'd like to see the tradition continued of doing what you think is right, each one having his own ideas of being an individual and not succumbing to public pressure.'" My cousin Ross, too bright-eyed, leans against me and has a brief convulsion. Once when, naïve and country-bred, we had traveled together to Capri, he had thought *he* would have to row the boat in the swirling waters to the Blue Grotto. Though he had not touched oars since a boyhood canoe trip on the Angelina, he was ready and game. I hold him now as at other similar times, clamping his tongue, and watch the little package under the sweet peas.

"'There is no typical student, or typical anything,'" quotes Harris. "'All that is typical is that all are different. They're all alike in that they're all different.'"

Making a sweeping, philosophical gesture to encompass "all," Harris's hand brushes the little box. He pauses a moment and looks down at it hard. He wipes his glasses and looks again. As though in silent prayer, he closes his eyes. When he touches the box again lightly, Sue nods at me; we know he has stuck the Phi Beta Kappa key and the flying bird decal back over the name, and made his decision. Behind her smile Sue looks pale. Sometimes the well one is sicker than the one who died.

Now Harris adds his own thoughts of Sister. "She dwelt in the realm of the expanded mind and knew all the important writings. She had a fantastic memory and an inquiring mind. She was especially interested in words, in their origins and derivations, their adaptions and adoptions to different societies and times, how with local usage their meanings change. She could take the least-known words and trace them to their beginnings. Phonetic and semantic changes, emotional coloring, loan and nonce words, were all part of her study. It was her wish to inspire, to motivate others, and some of us, privileged to know of her interests, have learned to share them."

As Harris repeats her, her, her, she, she, I think of M. Ventura getting into his car that fine April morning, thinking he was going somewhere else, some place cool, to Napoli Gardens on the shore, perhaps, never dreaming he was going to Claire, Texas, or that he would be cut off, like Hamlet's father, even in the blossoms of his sins—just another one of those who didn't even have time to say "Oh." Or had he a premonition, taking his morning shower in the glassed-in stall, sea horses and mermaids cavorting on the engraving, expensive but the wife liked it? Turning the knobs to cool, warm, cool, trying to get it just right, the water crashing on the misty, glazed glass, had he suddenly felt boxed in with all hell breaking loose? Did he know that he was being tailed, or had he thought, "At least it'll be safe in the car"?

Who had wired the bomb? Garfield, the Informer and Motor Man; the little girl waving from the window (Don't ever forget me, Daddy); the dog, a smart shepherd, wagging his tail, trying for a last pat, but stopping discreetly at the end of the walk? Or my seatmate on the plane, a childhood sweetheart of Mrs. V., who hadn't even bothered to come to the door to watch the pieces fly?

Sister speaks again. "'We have been changing since the beginning. Changes are cyclical, like stealing books.'" I think of Mr. Pard, stolen, in Channel Thirteen with the mouse, and of John Howard, the perpetrator, who in order not to give the fantasy away, and never believing I would find the real story, had made up the grasshopper chick and the ovipositor.

Cousin Ross straightens up and cannot remember the blackout.

"How did the health food pills work?" he asks.

"A real hit." He has forgotten that I wrote him. When Harris requests that we lift up our eyes to the hills in Sister's favorite psalm, mine go to the box beneath the sweet peas. I can almost hear it say, "This is ridiculous. These are not my ashes. When that damn turbulence threw things all over the plane and you spilled the only decent drink I've had in years on your seatmate, you picked up the wrong box. MLA stands for Mortician's Laymen Association, as improbable a little hobby group as you'll ever run into, and he's taking a sample of his work to show at Convention. Like the publishers all do with the lousy books they're pushing at the Modern Language or the Library meetings. Line 'em up in stalls in the lobby, fancy bindings and jackets on display while they wait for the cocktail parties. Get that Ninety-sixth Street bunk out of your head.

"My friend Ventura here died when he had his car checked at the wrong place, like by that idiot amateur in the TV ads. That dumb garageman put in a time bomb instead of working on the transmission. That's all. A similar question on explosives came up once at the reference desk.

The subject wasn't listed in *A Song for Occupations* and I had to research it.

"Your seatmate was just taking the remains to show what you can do with little pieces to work with. No matter how qualified, a person on any new job is afraid he'll do something wrong—screw the lid on too tight, put the carbon in backwards. Some even throw up. Your seatmate was just scared, even though he had nothing to worry about. Most ashes in the U.S. are not ashes at all but small bones, which don't rattle but won't burn either, and are a nuisance and environmental hazard if strewn. It's only in England and Europe, where the process is more advanced, that the bones are ground finely enough to be called ashes. But an explosion, such as M. Ventura had, plus the cremation, makes a first-rate pulverization.

"As for your pal, Pard, the Perpetrator, all he had to do to make up his great opus about grasshoppers, order Orthoptera, family Acrididae, was to look it up in the library catalog and go to the shelf: 632.72, right between 632.71 Thysanura (bristletails or silverfish) and 632.73 Pseudoneuroptera (dragonflies and thrips). Agriculturally speaking, that is. Zoologically he would go to 595.73. This is Dewey Decimal, of course. I don't count the Library of Congress.

"But what the hell difference does that or all this scurrying around trying to get the right ashes in the right hole make now? We're dead. Ventura got stuck down here and I have to go to another damn convention. C'est la vie."

"How about Heritage Club *Nana?*" asks Ross.

"Too loose to fit in the fireplace."

"I would like to close," says Harris, "with a quotation from an author she grew to love as a child. 'Do you think I could walk pleasantly and well-suited toward annihilation?' She was not afraid of death."

Not afraid, just didn't care for it, I think, and the service ends. "May the infinite mercy of an all-understanding Lord guide this dear, departed spirit home, may she rest in peace, the long journey ended."

At grave site the white box is placed between my mother's marker, a slab of plain gray granite placed here four years ago when she died at ninety-eight, and my father's tall column, the funerary style in 1910 when, aged thirty-three, he had died a month before my birth. ("I haven't given up hope yet," my mother, three years younger than he, had written him at the hospital. "I pray every minute that I'm alone. The children send love." Too young to die, too sick to live, he answered, "Whatever happens I will still be near you if it is possible in the scheme of things.") Sister remembers that at the funeral my mother, holding her three children close, had stood straight and dry-eyed by the grave. Sixty years later the death of a pet parakeet would leave her inconsolable. Skimming around the corners, he would fly into her room and land beside her on the bed where they would play "catch" with a tiny piece of paper wadded into a ball. "Kiss me, kiss me," he would cry, and, half-paralyzed, she would throw the ball to him with her good arm, until one day, off balance, she had rolled on him and killed him. "Kiss me, kiss me," he had cried, and my mother had bawled like a baby.

We had buried him in the butter dish.

My brother's sad grave is on the left of my mother's, by her first baby, Albert.

We stand in the open. The day before our arrival old friends cleaned off the plot. Many of the graves have no planting or flowers, as the loss from theft is great. The crape myrtle on my mother's grave is no longer there; the hawthorn never got a chance to root. They have even had to start locking their doors at night. But evidently no one will steal the plastic horrors, flowers so called, and they dot the flat graves of the cemetery. No "above entombment" is offered, unless here, as elsewhere, you count the everyday life of some not yet interred.

They are not much on cremation, either, though not precisely in the Bible Belt, and have not provided the customary little pup tent and campstools for the bereaved; the size of the hole does not warrant them. Nor have they air-conditioned the cemetery. Ambience gives way to sweat. Through the steam I see the Negro burying ground across the way, the North and the South Quarters of the Dead, still not integrated. Is it not enough that the dividing fence is removed? Here lies Cole, who made the bootleg shinny for my grandfather and buried it under the little field pea plants when the Texas Rangers came. Beneath a cedar tree is Grace, who was kind to my grandfather and called it the Tambourine Tree. Bliss, the cook, had moved to California.

And now in the steaming heat comes to me the smell of singeing cedar, for when she ironed the clothes from the black washpot, Grace cleaned her iron on a cedar sprig—giving off a spicy, pungent smell that, with the smell of tobacco spit sizzling on the hearth, turpentine poured into any wound, and yellow jessamine hanging from a creek-bank tree, makes up, with the Worcestershire–hog guts aroma, the everlasting smells of my childhood. But it's not singeing cedar that I smell, of course; it's a cigar sneaked in by the funeral assistant.

Harris, though respecting our views, does not compromise his own staunch religious faith, and intones the good-bye prayer: "We commit to mother earth the remains of her earthly garments . . . whose spirit is even now and evermore in God's gracious keeping." Finito (almost) for Sister, and visiting time under the trees with the old friends who have come to honor her. In a sort of friendly game not to reveal their names, they never give the secret away, and though I recognize many from my mother's funeral, have a rough time with some, bent and dried up like me. I, so lucky to be remembered by my childhood names, or by any name at all, am stumped by some of theirs. How about the old-lady kiss then, is it different here? Offhand, it appears to be more hugging here, except for the famous kissing cousins. But I can't say for sure, most present *are* old ladies and old men and on the whole as "with it" as I am. So far only one has asked, "Now was it you or your sister who died?"

While Sue and I thank them, the undertaker grows restless. He has another appointment but must stay till after we leave so he can lower the box into the hole in the ground—the final Finito. He tries to herd us to the cars; we resist, and while Harris stands guard over the white box, we walk among the graves, or on top of them, remembering. We find Grandmama Kay and Papa Scot. Separate in life, they are close in death, in need of weeding, and surrounded by their progeny, who seem to die a lot. We find the stone of my paternal great-grandmother, the original Keith, captured as a child by the Seminoles and freed (unwillingly, I wonder?) by my great-grandfather to be, a member of Andrew Jackson's Brigade. Cecil, an old friend, takes a picture of the name for me to show Kirby. A visiting cousin concentrates on more ancient dates; she wants to get into the Colonial Dames. I must remember to tell Sister that one for the Happy Hour; try to make her smile, but not too sorry she missed it.

We walk past the Mexican fighter, Pappy, who has a special marker on his grave, then we wander back to the new, uncovered hole, past my paternal grandmother and grandfather, whom I had never known; the latter had lost an arm at Antietam and became, though it does not say so on his tombstone, the best left-handed one-armed doctor in town. Briefly I wonder where he got his gloves, or if he wore them at all in this very warm place. A sister "killed as a young woman when milking, hooked by the cow" (I quote from a family record), is not given a name or a grave, and as children we thought she had been thrown over the moon. We visit Hugh Senior's grave and those of the two children born dead. Kneeling, my cousin removes a sprig of grass from one of the graves. For a moment she is still, hands on the hot earth, as if it were skin.

We are back at the plot. Cecil takes pictures of the little box for George. So it will not look so desolate, waiting by the hole, we spread the sweet peas around it.

Now it is time to go back to my cousin's for lunch and more visiting. Falling behind the lingering group, Sue and I take a last calculating view of the plot—room for two more—and walk on slowly toward the cars. Sue does not look back, and for a moment only three are left at the grave—Harris, me, and another bent, dried-up old lady. She looks vaguely familiar—some old muscle twitch, some quick gesture, an old dead-eye aim, an unusual bottle shape above the waist. Unlike the others, she throws out a clue with the hug.

"I always thought she was such a smart little devil, learning all those poems and skipping all those grades. Even if she couldn't keep up with me on the exercises."

Miss Roxie, elocutionist and croquet champ, releases me and leans over the grave. Still full of verve and vigor, she gives a forceful *Of the Open Road* flap of her hands. Harris and I watch as the Phi Beta Kappa key falls off again, lost in the sweet peas and revealing the engraved name. In perfect balance, Miss Roxie leans over closer and closer to study the name. And as in *Song of the Redwood-Tree*—

For know I bear the soul befitting me,
I too have consciousness, identity

—she performs her unforgettable arabesque. Beginning with a kind of open-stance harvest huddle, she melts into the catcher's squat, then with exquisite and natural grace terminates the movement in the pendulum swing. Years ago, viewed from behind the crape myrtle bush and between the grazing cows, it had been beautiful to me, and I had cried not only for the doomed Redwood-Tree, but for all the rocks and mountains, and all the earth, with their identity.

Indeed, since that long-ago day when, under the spell of her Smile-for-your-lover-comes magic, I had smiled like a fool and half risen to meet her (no telling what Mr. C.T. did on the hospital bed) I had come to have a lively respect for Miss Roxie and her gestures. Watching her, voluptuous, cool-breath'd, misty-topt, and tinged with blue, bear down on me that day on the porch steps, I had come, as had Mr. C.T., to believe that here was a fine, far-swooping, magnificent woman. I began to realize that all her interpretations were not muscular grotesques, that she was often more genuinely poetic in her embodiments than Sister, whose were all hard-core, sez-you, realism. When Whitman asked

Daughter of the lands, did you wait for your poet,
Did you wait for one with flowing mouth and indicative
hand

(a pretty good picture of Chuck Paramore when he took the negative side on Samuel Gompers) Sister would shake her head: No siree, she hadn't waited for *anybody*, let them wait for *her* (Chuck had gone by then). But Miss Roxie would stand still and move her lips as though in silent tribute to her poet, and end with a dark, brooding attitude.

Other of her interpretations possessed a certain ingrained sadness, a sensitive awareness of the injustices of life, a depth of honest feeling lacking in Sister's. But as my mother, always the compassionate realist, pointed out: you do not survive rickets as a child without a haunting memory of early sorrow—or lose $85,000 in a hotly contested will without bearing a deep, hurting scar.

But I often wondered if the same were not true of Miss Roxie as it was of Bart Raither and Papa Scot and even Eustace, who trained the mice to swim in synchronized flips: that she was doing this peculiar thing—Whitman with gestures—because she wanted to, and was hurting no one in doing so (except possibly Sister). Was she playing the fool for her own entertainment, I wondered, and laughing at herself as much as we were? I think she was having fun.

Bending over the grave now, she gives me no further clue.

"Little Ruth, what in the world does *Ventura* mean? Has Sister gone up there and married a dago?"

Now she is balanced almost on pointe on the edge of the hole. Seen from behind the crape myrtle, she had often seemed to be moon-pulled or tide-tilted, but in charge.

"Ventura's more than a name, Miss Roxie." Harris, who has never failed us yet, looks at me over her head and answers for me. "It means Come with God. Ventu Ra. Or some might say Wind of God. It's all the same. A mixture of Latin and Egyptian. May be some Coptic and Urdu in it. All it is, really, is a sacred blessing from ancient times. Like 'Mizrah,' or the 'Till We Meet Again' motif. Or just plain Good Luck, like 'Mazel Tov.'" He looks at her severely. "I'm surprised that with all your great reading and research in expression you never ran across something so well known. It was an everyday root word with Keith."

Miss Roxie gives him the rolling eye-ball; should she believe him or not? "Why, hon, I never knew the meaning of half those highfalutin words she tossed around. She kept me busy in the book."

And I like her immensely, and always have. With limited interest in the written word and the realm of the expanded mind, she could not have had an easy time with Sister for a pupil, even in so extracurricular a study as elocution. Even on the Camp Fire outings, trying to teach her to aim her pee straight as they stood around the gleaming campfire (Sister, bowlegged, would always go off center, counterclockwise), even then Miss Roxie had to admit it was slim victory she had over Sister. But there is a look in her eyes now: Skip, skip, skip, what's skip worth now? "Poor little thing," she says, "I sure didn't know she went up there and had to marry a dago.

"What's that damn funeral director up to?"

22

The funeral director is in the hearse shooting out exhaust fumes at us; we have tarried too long and displeased him. Angered, I am tempted to blow my whistle for the Ninety-sixth Street boys to dispatch him. George must never hear of this, but get instead the old placebo, perhaps true: Sister would have enjoyed every minute of it. Sleep well, then, Sister. You, too, M. Ventura. Don't forget, Sister, Ventura is a fine old name, whatever it means. Bear it proudly, wherever you go.

My cousin comes back to drive us to her house. I am tired and sad; my ribs hurt. I would like a drink—where could I get it? I had not remembered to bring "something" from Houston, and not even Harris, the inspired Urdu man, can help me here. It is a local-option town, voted so by godly folk, and the option is not to offer it to others if avoidable. In fact, a disturbing little custom is creeping in here. Called Afternoon Tea Party, it infringes on and often, by design, replaces the Happy Hour. I try to signal Sue for help, but she is walking head down, in apparent pain. Iced tea is the strongest I can expect now, and hard to beat in the heat, but no pain-killer. My cousin catches my arm as we walk past the other cars parked in the yard. At my mother's funeral it had been the showy Cadillac. Now it's the homely Mercedes-Benz. "Why don't you come live back down here where all your friends are?"

I stop a moment to lean on the gate. Others, by city ordinance, have taken down their gates and fences but my cousin has not. Hers is scrollwork iron from in front of my grandfather's house and the gate swings open a little even as on the day Mr. Percy sent it up the lane and we knew we had a new gate that wouldn't shut. Though called unpatriotic, my cousin would not give it up even for the scrap metal drive: surrender is not in her nature. Now it is covered with Maréchal Niels, those golden-yellow wonder roses that are scarce here, too, and is almost theatrically charming.

"Why do you stay up there in Harlem by yourself?"

My cousin is my friend. She loves me and does not intend to be unkind, or wrong. Stooped and arthritic, she looks at me with real concern.

Once, when aged thirteen and driving illegally (though there was no written statute as to age), we overturned our car (it was Buicks then) on a country road. Thrown free of the crash, my cousin had run three miles to get help for me and Sue and two other cousins pinned underneath, but not crushed by the car, which had caught on the bank of a gully. I remember looking from under the car, where I could move my eyes but not my head, to where she knelt to assure us that help was coming. Through the dripping black oil and the darts of light in my eyes, I could not see all of her. All I could see was a red spread on her drawers. Something had bit her hard, I thought, or a part of the car had hit her. The differential, I bet, if that's where it was (now I think it must have been the transmission). I tried to tell Sue this, but Sue, saturated with gas, was unconscious.

I tried to think how my sweet mama and grandmama would worry, what Papa Scot would do—his new big Buick he'd never really wanted till Mr. Percy said he did, in ruins. (Had Mr. Percy known it wouldn't take a curve with one person feeding the gas, another steering?) Would he make Worcestershire? Would he pass around the silver dollars at the funeral? Here, daughter, here, daughter, I'm proud of you? But all I could think about was that big spot of red.

It was only later that, all miraculously alive, we learned that the same day my cousin had run six miles (round trip) to save our lives she had become a dues-paying woman. It had been news to her, too.

It is a strong family that has never sought the popular or easy way. Hugh Senior, when he decided cases justly in favor of Negroes, had been shot at by disgruntled whites—dangerous, for he was an excellent marksman. On the local vote on the ruling of the Gaming Commission allowing paraplegics in wheelchairs to shoot at moving game, Hugh had been the only dissenter. When last year he died of his own shot, inflicted when the cancer finally ate through his jaw, some had been glad to see him go, among them, I imagine, a few paraplegics. But when Hugh Junior gives his environmental and anti-hunting lectures he is heard, if not heeded. When he does his needlepoint, he does it in public; there are no raised eyebrows—in his presence. Fearless, he took ballet lessons, opening up that almost forbidden dance form to all, as he had once helped open up the lunch counters. Even his four children are proud of him.

"I won't be alone," I tell my cousin. "Sue's sick and going home with me."

We walk on through the yard and past the great live oaks, and the flowering bushes that blaze in Azalea Trail time. We have just missed them. We climb the marble steps of my cousin's house, designed by my brother, and enter the "graciously appointed" rooms. My sister Sue smiles at me wanly and goes upstairs to lie down. I hope she has brought a little bottle from the plane; she seldom forgets. In the hall I am called to the telephone.

On the extension in the glassed-in back porch Detective Pickens is calling. And now I expect to hear it all: "He is not really crippled. He was never impoverished. He is a smart hood who was putting you on all the time. The jumping act is a tale as antiquated as Jack and the Beanstalk. He has never been in the South. Forget the porch steps act."

But I am wrong. Pard is dead. Trying to escape the police, led by Mr. Gamal to the building, he had tried to jump from one roof to the other when cornered. One of his feet had dragged and the shoelaces caught on a sculptured artisan under the decorative frieze.

His room had been full of children's books. A big steel file case held his running shoes, whistles, and appointment slips. No, he had not stolen the steel case, he had bought it from the stationery store for his Central Files. There was some whiskey. No dope.

"There's a package for you, Ruth," says Detective Pickens, and I remember the police do not call you Miss Last Name but by your first name.

"A book?"

"Looks like it. It's all wrapped up good, with your name on it and a note on an appointment card. It looks private."

"Read it, please," I say, as if he hasn't already, and he reads: "Sorry about all that, Mom. I'm not really bad, I'm just mean."

I wait a second. "Mr. Gamal?"

"His grandmother has sent for him, but he's fighting extradition."

Don't tell me, I know why: his grandmother is a severe, powerful, overbearing old woman who beat him as a child and ran the roost with an iron hand. Made him sit on the camel turds while she drank the champagne. He's scared to death of her.

How wrong can you be? I hang up the receiver and, resting my ribs on Hugh's needlepoint Wilderness Scene pillow (two eagles in midair, no dalliance, just winning the West—*again*) watch the mockers in the chinaberry tree. A family dispute is in progress.

In the parlor iced tea is tinkling in the cut glass (mind out, it might crack it). I hear the self-conscious laughter and muted talk of the Methodist wake. The smell of the baked ham and the fried chicken and the meat loaves, the fragrance of the okra fritters, fill the air. The homemade ice cream is waiting here, packed and ready for lunch. The dasher has already gone, and I should go, too.

But I watch the mocker, who has come a moment to balance on the wire by the porch steps. He gives me a one-sided account of the mix-up in the chinaberry—not *his* fault—gets no sympathy from me, and flies back to try again. Down past the chinaberry my cousin, a fern nut, has clustered varieties of them (105 grow in Texas) in the shade around a small pool, blue with sky. They have the damndest bluest skies here; someday they will run out of blue—then they will just go to the courthouse, look up all those leases and abstracts, drill, and find some more. The pool looks still and empty in the heat, but now and then, as though it fed through a bad filter, gurgles over the rocks. Something stirs. Could it be a frog moving up front? The herb garden, bordered by the mint for the iced tea, is in a cloistered shade beyond the sundial Hugh has designed in the shape of a triangular steel bird. The garden benches are here; the figs are in the back; they will have no fruit till July. In the fall the persimmons and pomegranates will bear their yellow and red balls back of the pole fence where the honeysuckle now drips. And drips.

I burn with envy. My cousin has the whole wonderful bit here, with the nicest back steps you've ever had your morning coffee on. It's all here, except the place where I want to live.

From the room voices come to me. "Isn't she a sight?" somebody says. "I hear she even brought a damn little old dead bird down here with her in that beat-up old bag."

Not to mention a nice little old mousie, sweetie pies, I think, and a mint-condition copy of *Atlas Shrugged* in Serbo-Croatian. I'm trembling. Who mourns the death of a thief, a mugger of old people, a potential killer? I do. I reject responsibility for his actions, but I mourn his death, as I do of all.

"You look like you need some iced tea, Little Ruth." My cousin comes to meet me as I make my way back to the parlor. "Why are you walking so stiff and so slow?"

"I fell down the steps. At home," I say.

"Then lean on me, precious."

I love them all, some of them, anyway, and when they say lean, you can lean without charge. Proud and lucky to be part of this family, I lean a little, and I thank them for everything, for love and friendship, for fritters (okra, eggplant, peach), and for all the extra things they do for people. But now I thank them for permission, gladly given, to leave quietly for my home. For I long for tomorrow when I can start back home with Sue, with my mouse and my dead warbler, back home to Harlem to my cats, my friends —Monica and her Toe Ties, Eddie Fuller and his filter, Nel Thompson and her funeral—back to my muggers, my dirt, my roaches, my jaybird, my three locks, Cookie Rothberg's words of wisdom, George's calls. (Whom else could he call now to prove he's still in the world, whom else could he tell his dreams to? Make like Miss Liberty, Georgie.)

I go back to Mr. Gamal, and to Sister. For Sister is not here. Sister's out skipping on the Open Road, Sister's at Convention. When my seatmate opens the syrup bucket in the big crowded showroom I hope he is not too humiliated. Many fine young exhibitors, hovering around their stalls, formaldehyde stinging their nostrils, their tender-skinned hands groping, jerking back when they touch the unknown, will, I hope, commend him for his trend toward Down Home simplicity. Isn't any but the lid and the container too much, more a bore? Sister, I hope, does not tell him a better way to do it, a process she read once when looking up a reference question, 393 point something in Dewey.

Sister had no choice. She went to Convention. For a while Sue and I are lucky. We can still choose. We can go home.

23

Now three weeks later, bourboned in the big blue, hostage of a cocksure pilot and an overworked stewardess, I fly again. Boxed in with the same old doubt and sadness, I carry different ashes. Sue, athlete extraordinaire, sister and friend, is dead. Another convention is on board the plane. My seatmate gives me a wary glance and nervously grasps his carry bag. I hold fast to the ashes, await the turbulence, and dread the morrow.

Why go, then? Because the hole is there and one must follow the hole? Is a hole like a star? Hitch your wagon to, wish upon, would I were steadfast as thou art, twinkle, twinkle? Is this golf, where filling the empty hole is the aim of the game? Why not keep the ashes at home by the sofa where they can work the crossword puzzles, watch the TV stories and ball games, sing their little songs, and delight with their wit? Because they're ashes, and the others are already in their holes there, row upon row, expecting them, waiting for them? Because M. Ventura is lonesome for news from Queens? Because the dead have no rights?

Sue, the last of my immediate family, is gone. But I am not alone. Found in the mailbox this morning with Con Edison, Citibank, Pen Pal (he's won another contest), and all the begs and endangered species, was a message. In a plain stamped envelope with no return address, written on a six-months appointment pad, it reads:

Dear Ruth:

I have taken over the work of John Howard, or Pard, as you may know him, and wish to assure all those he served of our continuing solicitude. His death was a shock to our whole club, and it has required some few weeks to restructure our organization. As you know, he was Head, or as he modestly put it, Backup Man, and this position is by unanimous vote now mine. I hope to fill it with the same efficiency and imagination as he.

However, to provide adequate space in which to update our Central Files and expand our community services, the Club is in need of a new base of operations.

In short, I want a free place to stay.

I would, of course, work for my board. I am good with old ladies and cats (to the present have drowned few and thrown only the most uncooperative out the window), put in fuses, feed birds, grow plants (you need a special H_2J_4 fertilizer on that palm tree; I make it myself), haul out garbage, fix filters, paint walls, reupholster furniture, cut cats' claws, train mice, roach-sit, deliver packages, copy signatures, answer pen pals, smile when I jog, quote Whitman (with or without gestures), sweeten sour sopranos, and stop flushing toilets (Let the water be still: no miracle, I'm a plumber, though without portfolio). As Backup Man to the Former Head Backup Man, I am proficient in the manipulation of elevators, anything electric, Celsius, and unlisted telephone numbers, but consider this last contrary to tenets of the First Amendment.

I guarantee I will not say You know, Take care, No way, Have a good day, Get back to you, or He's got class, do not think Keith is all that unusual a name for a woman, or Martha or Evelyn for cats.

I will not try to put anybody on a white wine and honey, less-grease, or natural foods diet (all food's natural if it's natural for you to like it; my pig's-feet quiche with yogurt is a case in point). By absolutely respecting each other's privacy and right to act as they choose without hurting others, I think we'll make it. And at the risk of throwing the final cornball—isn't freedom of choice what it's all about? With that in mind, I've taken the liberty of choosing to employ, to help us as needed, a small boy, quite old for his age really—youth seems to mature earlier and earlier these days—who lives handily in the apartment below us.

If you don't like the name Jesus or Honey, just call me Robin. Like Sister says, there's not just one, another one will always be there waiting.

All God's chillun got chillun, Mom.

My seatmate clutches his carryall and stares out the window. The tilting wing stares back, then jerks to the left. The *Fasten your seat belts* sign flashes on. I fold my letter and file it in the up-chuck bag.

Am I going back to this? Of course. It's where I live. And Robin Redbreast is waiting. So are Detective Pickens, and Mr. Gamal, and all *their* chillun.

And the right to choose, even if it's dangerous.

But now for the turbulence.

Alma Stone was born in the small East Texas town of Jasper. She has had short stories published in *The Yale Review*, *The Antioch Review*, the *American Literary Anthology* and the *O. Henry Prize Stories*. Her novels include *The Banishment*, *The Bible Salesman*, and *The Harvard Tree*. Ms. Stone is a longtime resident of New York City's Upper West Side.